PUFFIN B

THE PUFFIN BOOK OF CHRISTMAS STORIES

Following their successful anthology for younger readers, *Round the Christmas Tree*, Sara and Stephen Corrin now bring us this delightful collection of Christmas stories for older children. From Charles Dickens's archetypal *A Christmas Carol* to the Breton legend of *Brother Johannick and his Silver Bell*, from Leon Garfield's touching tale *The Forbidden Child* to the wit and humour of Thomas Hardy's *The Thieves who Couldn't Help Sneezing*, this is a book full of Christmas fun and laughter, enchantment and wonder.

Sara and Stephen Corrin are the editors of many popular anthologies for children. Sara was born within the sound of Bow Bells and has all the cockney's good humour and jaunty repartee. She travels considerably, telling stories, especially in children's libraries, and has made the subject of children's responses to literature one of her main studies. Stephen Corrin was brought up on a mixed diet of the *Gem*, the *Magnet*, the Bible, cricket and Beethoven quartets. He reviews, writes stories and translates from French, Russian, German and Danish.

EDITED BY SARA AND STEPHEN CORRIN

The Puffin Book of *Christmas* —Stories—

Illustrated by Jill Bennett

PUFFIN BOOKS
IN ASSOCIATION WITH FABER AND FABER

for Tom

Puffin Books, Penguin Books Ltd, Harmondsworth, Middlesex, England
Viking Penguin Inc., 40 West 23rd Street, New York, New York 10010, U.S.A.
Penguin Books Australia Ltd, Ringwood, Victoria, Australia
Penguin Books Canada Limited, 2801 John Street, Markham, Ontario, Canada L3R 1B4
Penguin Books (N.Z.) Ltd, 182–190 Wairau Road, Auckland 10, New Zealand

First published by Faber and Faber Limited 1984
Published in Puffin Books 1986

Made and printed in Great Britain by
Cox & Wyman Ltd, Reading
Typeset in Meridien

CONTENTS

INTRODUCTION

"Some say, that ever 'gainst that season comes
Wherein our Saviour's birth is celebrated,
The bird of dawning singeth all night long;
And then, they say, no spirit dare stir abroad;
The nights are wholesome; then no planets strike,
No fairy takes, nor witch hath power to charm,
So hallow'd and so gracious is the time"
 (Shakespeare's lovely lines in *Hamlet*).

The legends that have grown up around the deeply spiritual theme of Christmas are at the heart of this collection. But radiating from this centre are countless and varied moods which mirror the mystery and joyousness of Yuletide.

The spirit of Christmas says many things to different people: Good cheer, good will, good vittles and good fun. But its *true* spirit, in whatever way one chooses to present it, must reflect our desire to be a little nobler than our all-the-year-round earthy selves; perhaps at this page of the calendar we feel the need to provide a little nourishment for our souls.

The strange and wondrous events that surround the Christmas Story fill us with awe and stimulate our explorations into the supernatural. Christmas, for one reason or another, has traditionally become the season for stories: the spirits, indeed, may not "stir abroad" but they do make their appearance all the same in stories, told or read, around the festive hearth or tree.

7

CHRISTMAS WITH THE CHRYSTALS

Noel Streatfeild

"Dear Mum, I saw the enclosed and thought it might suit you and Dad. Love, Ivy." The enclosed was an advertisement which read:

Wanted: married couple to take complete charge of kitchen for Christmas. Castle has been rented for large party including several children. Write Box 2060.

Mrs Chrystal read the advertisement at breakfast, and passed it across to her husband, Ted Chrystal.

"I never thought when I wrote to Ivy saying we might take temporary domestic work we'd be away for Christmas."

Ted always thought well before he spoke.

"Nor me neither," he agreed at last, "but I don't see no harm in us writing in. We're used to working of a Christmas, you know, Rosa."

Rosa took back the advertisement.

"In our own line, yes, but fancy us spending all Christmas in a kitchen, seem funny, wouldn't it?"

There was another pause, during which Ted slowly finished his cup of tea.

"I don't know so much. We've always tried to give kids a good time of a Christmas and this is another way of doing it. You're a beautiful cook, Rosa, and, though I say it as shouldn't, you couldn't want a better kitchen help than your humble."

Rosa looked rather like an old-fashioned cottage loaf, for

she had an almost round body. Now she heaved herself out of her chair, and balanced herself on her short fat legs.

"Whatever you say, Ted, you know that. I'll get the inkpot and write straight away."

Three days later the Chrystals got a reply to their letter. It was written on very grand stiff cream note-paper, with a London address and telephone number at the top.

Dear Mrs Chrystal,
    I am instructed by Mrs Cornelius to reply to your application. You will please both call at the above address on Monday next at 12 noon precisely.
Yours sincerely,
F. SMITH
(*Secretary*).

"I don't know, Ted," said Rosa, "that I like the sound of this. There's something about that twelve noon precisely that I don't fancy."

Ted took the letter, read it, and held it up to the light to see the watermark in the paper. Then he passed it back to Rosa.

"I know what you mean and maybe I don't fancy it myself, but where that paper come from there's money, and we can do with a bit of that, so we'll be there at twelve noon precise come Monday."

Mrs Cornelius lived in an immensely expensive block of flats not far from Piccadilly. Rosa had on her fur coat, a left-over from better-off days. The fur had an out-all-night look, and the coat no longer met in front, so it had to be worn open, but, as Rosa said to Ted, "fur gives confidence." Under the coat she wore what she called "me velvet". This was a plum-coloured dress which had been good once but now, at important places, had a bald look. On her head she wore a small black hat trimmed with a shiny buckle. Ted had on his only suit, steamed and pressed for the occasion, his better shirt carefully pruned by Rosa of threads round the collar and cuffs, and his overcoat. They were not proud of the overcoat, which was definitely past its prime, so it had been their plan to leave it in the hall of the flats while they saw Mrs Cornelius, but the uniformed commissionaire was so terrifically grand and aloof they lost their nerve, and having given the flat number, meekly followed him into the lift, Ted still wearing the coat.

Some women can never make the place where they live look like a home. Others, even if they only spend a night in a room give it a belonging atmosphere. Mrs Cornelius was the first sort of person. Her sitting-room was enormous, with a lovely view from the windows of Green Park. Everything she possessed was rare and expensive; some pieces of her furniture and many of her ornaments should have been in a museum. Every chair and the sofa had cushions without a dent in them, so it was hard to believe anyone sat down. The exquisite desk, though there was a chair in front of it, was obviously never used. In great vases, though it was December, there were formal arrangements of forced spring flowers, which seemed to droop from lack of affection.

Ted and Rosa, having been shown in by a pompous man-servant, waited until the door shut, then they gave each other a look.

"This isn't us, Ted," Rosa whispered, "no money wouldn't be worth it."

Ted answered, for him, quite quickly.

"Shouldn't wonder if you're right, old girl. Pity, we could have done with the money, but it just wouldn't be worth it if we was scared to touch anything."

A woman came in. She was small, thin, mouse-coloured all over, and nervous as a bird scared, though it is hungry, to pick up a crumb. She spoke in a low, frightened voice.

"Mr and Mrs Chrystal? I'm Miss Smith, Mrs Cornelius's secretary."

"Pleased, I'm sure," said Rosa.

Ted gave a faint bow.

"Good morning, Miss."

"Mrs Cornelius is seeing you herself." Miss Smith stated this as if she was telling the Chrystals they were to see the Queen.

11

Her tone gave Rosa courage.

"I don't think we'll be troubling her, thank you." She was going to explain that she and Ted liked nice things round them, but homely, when she was stopped in the middle of a word by Miss Smith, whose face was wobbling as faces do before the owner cries.

"Oh, please don't say no. I oughtn't to tell you this, but you're the only answer we've had, and we've been advertising for ages, and it's almost Christmas, and how I'm going to manage the castle on my own . . ." The wobble won, tears began rolling down Miss Smith's mouse-coloured face.

"Now, dear," said Rosa, "don't take on."

Ted made shocked clucking noises.

"Maybe we spoke hasty. Mrs Chrystal and me have never been ones to let others down."

Miss Smith dabbed her eyes.

"So stupid, but you've no idea what is planned, you see . . ." She broke off, turning grey under the mouse colour. "Here is Mrs Cornelius. Please, please don't tell her I was upset, or what I've said."

Mrs Cornelius was a woman who might have been seventy, but her face, hair and teeth had for years been so regardlessly looked after and operated on that she could have been younger. She wore a black dress which appeared simple, but an experienced eye would have told it could not have cost less than a hundred pounds. She had wonderful pearls round her neck and a magnificent emerald ring on her finger, and emeralds in her ears. It was not, however, at these things or the frock at which the Chrystals looked, but at Mrs Cornelius's eyes. These were a startlingly vivid blue and hard as a calculating machine. Mrs Cornelius had a voice to match her eyes.

"Are these the couple, Miss Smith?" Miss Smith made a sound which could have been yes. Mrs Cornelius came into the room and sat down. She pointed to the sofa. "You may sit."

Gingerly Ted and Rosa sat, terribly conscious as they did so of the dents their behinds were making in the otherwise

uncreased sofa. Ted could feel Rosa was nervous and that gave him the courage to be the first to speak.

"My wife is a good cook, but we were just saying to Miss Smith here we were not at all sure we'd be right for this post . . . "

Mrs Cornelius apparently did not hear that.

"I must explain the position for which I may engage you. I have married three times. I gave my first husband a daughter before he died. That daughter is now married, a very poor marriage, I fear. She has two children. My second marriage was to an American. I gave him a son before he died; that son is now dead, but there is a widow with one child. Mr Cornelius came from South Africa; I gave him a son who is married and has three children. It is many years since I saw my own children, I have never seen my son-in-law nor my two daughters-in-law nor my grand-children, so this year I propose to see them all. I have rented Caldecote Castle, which is in Kent, and I am entertaining them for Christmas. You will cook for the household."

Rosa had been counting on her fingers while Mrs Cornelius was speaking.

"That would mean eleven to cook for, as well as yourself and Miss Smith, making thirteen."

"That is correct," Mrs Cornelius agreed, "But as well there will be Mr Cornelius."

That surprised both Ted and Rosa, who had taken it for granted Mr Cornelius was as dead as were the other two husbands. Rosa looked round for signs of him, for in her opinion you could always tell when there was a man in the house. She could not see anything male about, but she felt that there was a Mr Cornelius somewhere was good news, for it meant, if they took the job, there would be someone else to work for besides Mrs Cornelius.

"That makes a difference, doesn't it, Ted?"

Mrs Cornelius turned the full blaze of her eyes on Rosa.

"I cannot imagine why Mr Cornelius should make a difference, for it is many years since we met."

There was a pause, while Rosa and Ted digested that. Then Ted said, "Fourteen plus staff I suppose."

"Dailies only, so no meals," Mrs Cornelius stated firmly.

Ted shook his head, for he was by now determined not to allow his Rosa to endure Mrs Cornelius.

"All the same, it'll be too much for the wife." He got up. "I'm sorry we've taken up your time. Come along, Rosa."

Miss Smith gave a sound between a sob and a moan. Rosa, as she heaved herself up from the soft depths of the sofa, looked at her with compassion.

"Don't take on, dear, but fourteen is a lot and we're not as young as we were."

Mrs Cornelius gave Miss Smith a look which, had she seen it, would have shrivelled her.

"Be quiet you foolish creature." She held up a hand. "One moment, you two. I realize the work will be hard, so if you are willing to go to the castle on Friday next to prepare and lay in stores, and to remain until the 28th, I will pay you over and above all expenses one hundred pounds."*

One hundred pounds! To Rosa and Ted that was a fortune, magic money which others had but never you. Why, however hard the work, with a hundred pounds they could afford to get over it with a little holiday. Ted nudged Rosa to show she should answer.

"Very well, Mrs Cornelius, if you would put the offer in writing, we'll come."

Miss Smith and the Chrystals arrived together on the following Friday. The castle, they discovered, though it was partly lived in sometimes by the owners, was mostly a museum, and it is difficult to make museums homely for a Christmas party. Mrs Cornelius was using only one wing, but that had thirty bedrooms, a vast drawing-room, a dining-room, which looked as though it should have belonged to a city company, a billiard room, and many smaller rooms. It had, too, a great central staircase and long passages most inadequately heated.

*In 1958, when this story was written, £100 was worth a great deal more than it is today.

"The temperature in Mrs Cornelius's part of the castle is never to drop below seventy degrees," said Miss Smith through chattering teeth.

Rosa had her own troubles with a great draughty kitchen, but she still had kindness to spare for Miss Smith.

"You can only do your best, dear. I reckon if you get the chill off the place it'll be a miracle."

But it is wonderful what can be done when there is unlimited money to spend, and by midday on Saturday there were fires in every fireplace, and oil stoves in chilly corners, and an old man who lived nearby was bribed at an enormous wage to do nothing but keep the stoves and fires going.

Miss Smith contrived other miracles. Nobody wants to work over Christmas, especially not housewives with their own families to think of, but Christmas is an expensive time, and so Miss Smith, with persuasion and offering unheard-of pay, organized a small regiment of women willing to work in shifts starting on the Monday morning.

Rosa and Ted would not have any help as they felt there would have to be a good deal of muddling through, and if that was to happen they would rather it was when there was no one watching. One of their troubles was the food. Rosa prided herself on her cooking, but some of the things sent for the store cupboard she had never heard of or seen before. There were tins of strange tropical fruits. There were great chunks of dried turtle – looking for all the world like blocks of amber. Did people really drink soup made of kangaroos' tails? They had, of course, heard of *paté de foie gras*, but how did you serve it? The same applied to caviare; never had Rosa supposed caviare was sold in such enormous tins. Then there were cases of Christmas delicacies. Was the cook expected to arrange all the exotic little eats, and, if so, on what?

"Thank God I brought my *Mrs Beeton*," Rosa confided to Ted; "if I'm properly stuck she'll see me through."

Mrs Cornelius arrived in the morning. Until she came into the castle there had been a happy bustle as Miss Smith's first shift of women came in and began cleaning and polishing.

The women knew each other, and there were jokes and whistling and snatches of singing. But the moment Mrs Cornelius came in it was as if the icy wind from outside came with her. She made a tour of inspection, and though she said very little, and even gave a word of praise – "Your arrangements appear satisfactory, Miss Smith" – as she went round the castle, the Christmas feeling seemed to slip out through the doors and windows.

Rosa and Ted had by now made the kitchen their home. It was gay with Christmas cards, for another large batch had arrived that morning, and Ted had found some holly in the grounds and had stuck branches over the clock and on the dresser. Then there was Rosa's old thumbed *Mrs Beeton* on the table, and Rosa's large overalls hanging on the kitchen door. So it was not into an unlived characterless room that Mrs Cornelius stepped when she visited the kitchen, but into a warm, rich-smelling place, full of atmosphere.

Rosa and Ted had been practising for that moment, and though they had laughed a lot they had it planned to perfection.

"Good morning, Madam, welcome to Caldecote Castle," said Ted with a deep bow.

Rosa, for all her cottage-loaf shape, managed a bob of a curtsy.

"And the compliments of the season, Madam; I hope you have a wonderful Christmas."

This welcome sounded so like a scene from an old-fashioned play that Mrs Cornelius gave each of the Chrystals a look from her hard blue eyes to see if the welcome was intended as insolence. But it clearly was not, for both Rosa and Ted returned her look with expressions of such goodwill it was obvious, odd though it might seem, that they meant what they had said.

Mrs Cornelius did not reply to the goodwill wishes, but they did something to her, for she did not say the words that had been on her lips when she came in: "Take down those cards and that holly. This is a kitchen, not an amusement arcade." Instead she went straight to giving her orders.

17

"I shall have a light lunch. All my guests will be here for tea. Miss Smith has, I believe, given you the menu for dinner tonight?"

"Yes, Madam," said Rosa.

"Then that I think is all." Mrs Cornelius turned to go, but Rosa stopped her.

"What about the children?"

"What about them?"

"Well, children won't be eating oysters and that at eight o'clock like you've ordered," Rosa explained. "Are they to have supper, or something to their tea?"

It was so long since Mrs Cornelius had met a child, and even her own she had never seen eat that she could remember, so she did not know what Rosa meant.

"Something to their tea? What can you have for tea other than cake, scones and sandwiches?"

Ted saw he must help Rosa.

"Miss Smith told us the eldest child is fourteen and the youngest seven; that means special food, Madam, and a sit-down tea."

"A glass of milk and biscuits or that for the little ones in bed," Rosa added, "but something light but tasty for the others, they won't want to upset their stomachs with what's going into the dining-room."

Mrs Cornelius looked and felt as if she was having something unpleasant told to her.

"I am really not interested in what or when the children eat. I will instruct Miss Smith to find out from the parents what is required and she will inform you."

Once more Rosa and Ted managed the bow and bob they had rehearsed. Then, as the door closed behind Mrs Cornelius, Rosa covered her mouth with her hand to hold back the big laugh that rose like a fountain in her.

"She'll be the death of me, Ted."

Ted's eyes were twinkling.

"Come on, my old trouble, for she'll be the death of both of us if her light lunch isn't served pronto."

Virginia, the daughter Mrs Cornelius told the Chrystals she had given her first husband, had, by her mother's standards, made a poor marriage. For she had married Tom Oswald, who not only had no money of his own, but was not much good at earning it. Mrs Cornelius, when Virginia had collected sufficient courage to tell her whom she was marrying, had been so disgusted she had refused to attend the wedding, and had not seen Virginia since. But though her mother might think Tom Oswald a poor sort of husband, Virginia knew him to be a perfect one, for he was warm, loving, and of a happy disposition, all qualities she had been unused to in her own home. Tom was a gardener, a job that was not well paid but at which he was very good. Where Tom gardened there was a cottage, and in it Virginia's and Tom's children, Alan and Benita, had grown up to the ages of fourteen and twelve without ever seeing or thinking about their Cornelius grandmother.

It had been one of the few mornings that the Oswalds' cottage had not been full of laughter when the invitation arrived to spend Christmas in Caldecote Castle. Tom and Virginia, for the sake of the children, tried not to show how depressed and frightened the letter of invitation made them, but they were not successful, for Alan and Benita were intelligent.

"Must we go?" Alan asked. "She's never bothered with us before."

"Christmas is always perfect here," Benita pleaded. "Don't let's go."

Mrs Cornelius would not have believed her ears if she could have heard Tom's answer to his children.

"Poor old lady. We mustn't be selfish, we have so much and she's got nothing. Let's give her one nice Christmas to remember."

Mrs Cornelius's second husband had been a Mr Silas P. Dawson, an American. By him she had a son called James. Mr Dawson had been immensely rich and it had been his intention that James should be rich too, but he had died while

19

James was a small child and so had left his fortune to his wife, expecting her to provide for James. And so she would have done if James had behaved as she expected him to. But James had not, for he had fallen in love with a pretty penniless school teacher, and insisted on marrying her, and a year later had died, leaving behind him a baby son called Gardiner. Mrs Cornelius felt that James's death relieved her of responsibility. "That girl Lalla he married," she told herself, "supported herself as a teacher before she married him, so I suppose she can continue to do so. I will, however, provide for Gardiner in my will."

That keeping yourself as a school teacher was one thing, and keeping yourself and a baby son was another had not struck Mrs Cornelius, and Lalla, who was proud, would not write to explain and ask for help. Instead, somehow she managed, and though she and Gardiner lived in two rooms in down-town New York, which were far too hot in summer and dismally cold in winter, they not only managed to survive but to enjoy themselves.

Gardiner had scarcely heard of Grandmother Cornelius, but he was wild with excitement at the thought of the journey by jet plane, which was part of the invitation.

"Gee, a jet plane! Will that be something to tell the other boys!"

Mrs Cornelius's living husband, old Hans Cornelius, lived outside Cape Town in an exquisite white Cape Dutch house. Just a couple of miles away his son Jan lived in another beautiful house with his wife Anna and their three children, Peter who was ten, and the two little girls, Jane who was eight and Rinke seven.

Christmas comes in the summer in South Africa, so when Jan drove over with Ann to show his father their letter from Mrs Cornelius, they found him in his rose garden, which was in full flower.

Old Hans smelt a glorious golden rose before he gave his opinion.

"I would like to say no. Why should we leave our beautiful

South Africa to go to cold foggy England? But your mother, Jan, is no longer young and no doubt lonely, so if you can make the sacrifice, Anna, my dear, I think we should all go, for it will be a treat for her to see your children."

The families arrived at the castle within half an hour of each other. The first to get there were Gardiner and his mother. Miss Smith, trying by the warmth of her smile to build her small mouse-coloured self into a whole reception committee, met them in the hall and showed them to their rooms, and, as she did so, her spirits bounded upwards. For in Lalla she saw not a frightening, demanding American daughter-in-law belonging to Mrs Cornelius, but a tired young woman, with a face prematurely lined from standing too long hours in the store where she worked, and with hair turning grey from the worry of making ends meet. And so Miss Smith did something she had never dreamed she would be doing to one of the daughters-in-law, she put an arm through Lalla's and said: "You must rest while you are here. I shall see you have breakfast in bed every day."

Alan and Benita, as soon as they arrived, were turned out of their rooms by their mother who, looking at the vast amount of cupboard space, had decided she would unpack for the family, and so, by skilful laying out and hanging up, disguise how few clothes they possessed. So Gardiner, prowling along a passage, ran slap into them.

"'Lo," he said, pleasantly surprised by Alan's appearance, for he had on his grey flannel trousers and he had supposed all English boys wore short pants. "I'm Gardiner. You'll be Alan and Benita. Gee, this is a big place and unfriendly some way."

"Have the others come, the South African ones?" Benita asked.

Gardiner dismissed the Cornelius children.

"Naw. Come on, let's explore."

It was exploring that took Alan, Benita and Gardiner into the kitchen. They reached it by way of the thickly carpeted front hall, where every corner was set with formally staged groups of pot plants.

21

"Like a funeral parlour," Gardiner whispered. "How say we see what's through this green door?"

To the children the kitchen was immediately home. Rosa and Ted were having an early cup of tea, and without invitation the three pulled up chairs and joined them.

"How come," Gardiner asked, looking appreciatively at the cards and holly, "You've got all this out here and we've got nothing back there?"

Rosa passed him a cup of tea.

"You're seeing your Granny after tea. I'm sure you've only got to ask and she'll send for a tree and holly and that."

Benita, relaxing for the first time since she had reached the castle, took the slice of cake Ted offered her.

"It's not that we need a tree exactly, but it's not like Christmas without one. At home Dad cuts down a tree and we all decorate it."

"I daresay your Dad could do the same here," said Ted, "there's plenty of trees in the grounds."

Alan shook his head.

"I don't reckon Dad would face up to that. Out there," he pointed vaguely towards the front of the castle, "it's like a posh hotel, you couldn't mess it up, and you can't trim a tree without mess."

The Cornelius children might be small but they were bright. So while their mother was unpacking, cheeping like sparrows and as if they had always known the castle, they hurried along the bedroom corridor, down the main staircase, through the baize-covered door which divided the kitchen world from the rest of the house, straight to Rosa, Ted and their new cousins. They stood in the doorway, beaming.

"Hullo," said Peter, "I'm Peter, this is Jane and this is Rinke. We're hungry."

Rosa fetched some more cups from where they were hanging on the dresser.

"Bring up three chairs, Ted. Do you drink milk or tea, dears?"

When the children were fetched by Miss Smith to come to the drawing-room, something made the six know they must

22

not tell Grandmother Cornelius that they had made friends with the Chrystals. Instead they told her about each other, to the great amusement of old Hans Cornelius, who was watching Mrs Cornelius's face.

After they had all been introduced Rinke said, "Do you know, Grandmother Cornelius, Benita's father is a gardener, which means they can have all the vegetables they need, which is lucky, for they can't often have meat."

"Imagine that," Jane added. "We have meat every day, don't you, Grandmother Cornelius?"

"Gardiner's mother works in a store," Peter piped up, "so Gardiner's always had to get his own lunch. He makes sandwiches of anything that's in the ice box; when there isn't much he makes do with bread."

Gardiner thought that was enough about him. He jerked his head towards the three Cornelius children and gave a wink.

"They were wondering how Santa gets to find his way in a place this size, but I told them he'd figure it out, that's right, isn't it?"

"We were wondering about a tree, Grandmother Cornelius," Benita said softly. "I mean, it needn't cost anything, I'm sure there's one about Dad could cut down."

"And we could make the ornaments," Alan suggested hopefully, "fir cones and that painted."

Mrs Cornelius, who had been silenced by the shower of talk, made a signal to Miss Smith.

"Order a tree and tell them to send decorations, and people to hang them up."

"And there ought to be masses and masses of parcels in coloured paper," Jane prompted, "there always are."

Mrs Cornelius had not had a Christmas present for so long she had forgotten about them. She gave another signal to Miss Smith.

"And order parcels suitably packed."

Twelve eyes stared at her. Rinke spoke for them all.

"That," she said firmly, "is not the way to buy Christmas presents. You choose them."

Gardiner looked round the beautifully furnished but unlived-in room.

"Don't you get cards at Christmas, Grandmother Cornelius?"

Miss Smith caught old Hans Cornelius's eye. It said: "That's enough for one night. Take them away." Miss Smith took the hint.

"Come along, dears. It's time you younger ones went to bed," and she swept the children out of the room.

The grown-ups' dinner having been served and washed up, the Chrystals, Alan, Benita and Gardiner sat down to their own supper. A splendid meal where everybody ate something different, and all helped themselves. And it was then that the children learned something strange. It came out when Rosa and Ted were showing them their Christmas cards.

"Why," Benita asked, "does this one say 'To the best goose that ever laid a golden egg'?"

Ted looked at Rosa, who smiled cosily back at him.

"Tell them. They won't say anything and they'll like to hear."

"Well, it's this way," said Ted. "I've been an actor all my life."

"And none better," put in Rosa.

"But my speciality was animals."

"More especially geese," said Rosa. "I reckon there's never been a goose in panto to touch him."

Rosa and Ted, helped out by Alan and Benita, had to explain to Gardiner what a pantomime was, and then he found it hard to believe there were such entertainments.

"The mother's a man called a dame, the principal man is played by a girl, and you come on as a goose. I haven't seen nothing yet!"

It was with difficulty Rosa and Ted urged the children to bed, for they knew they must be tired, and they themselves had a long, hard day ahead of them.

"I tell you what, though," said Rosa, "to-morrow I'll get Miss Smith to buy paper for making paper rings; we always had them when I was a child."

"That's right," Ted agreed, "smashing decorations they make."

"Even the little ones can make them," Rosa went on, "and while you're doing it Ted shall tell you about working in a pantomime."

To the dismay of the adults the next day was hopelessly wet, so wet that even the men could only manage a short walk in the dripping castle grounds. But the children did not mind how much it rained. All the morning they were busy, helping to prepare the lunch; then when they had eaten a splendid meal themselves, the paper for ring-making arrived and they settled round a table with a vast pot of paste made by Rosa, and Ted sat with them, talking in his slow way about pantomimes. Sometimes he demonstrated.

"Then I'd come to the footlights, like this; wonderful music I had for that bit, and acted like I was heart-broken, see, for I was turned out, me that was part of the family."

Rosa hummed Ted's goose music, and Ted, in spite of the fact that he was wearing ordinary trousers help up over his shirt by braces, and an apron tied round him, seemed to the children to become a goose.

During tea, Ted, helped out by Rosa, imitated principal boys they had known, and to see him swaggering up and down the kitchen as if he was a lovely girl with magnificent legs in tights was really something. So it was to a kitchen echoing with laughter that Miss Smith came from the sad bridge-playing drawing-room to fetch the children to see their grandmother. It was after this visit that they decided to keep their decorations a secret.

"Good evening, children," said Mrs Cornelius. "What have you been doing to-day?"

The children had not planned what to answer if they were asked that, so Peter said, "Playing."

"When is the tree being erected?" Mrs Cornelius asked Miss Smith.

"Now," Miss Smith twittered. "It can be lighted to-night."

"Trees," said Jane, "aren't lighted until Christmas Eve.

That's when you have your presents."

Alan disagreed with that.

"We don't have ours till Christmas Day."

"We don't get a tree," Gardiner broke in. "Mum can't afford one."

In the little silence that fell after that old Hans Cornelius looked at Mrs Cornelius.

"We wouldn't have one either if Dad didn't get it free," said Benita.

On the way back to the kitchen the children had a small committee meeting.

"Let's keep our rings for the kitchen part of the castle," Peter suggested, "It's much the nicest bit."

Alan had another idea. "And I'll find a little tree in the grounds, there's heaps of room for it at the end of the kitchen."

The Chrystals were delighted when they heard what was planned.

"Oh, I would like a tree," said Rosa, "it's years since I had one. And I tell you what we'll do, we'll put the lights out on Christmas Eve and light the tree and leave the curtains undrawn; they say you should always have lights in the window on a Christmas Eve to show the Christ-Child the way."

Rinke put her arms as far as they would go round Rosa.

"Darling, darling Rosa, could we sing carols round your tree?"

"It's the only place we could," Alan pointed out; "carols would sound all wrong in any other part of the castle."

The tree, decorated quietly and efficiently by girls and men sent with it, was lit that evening. When it was finished, Miss Smith, who had long ago become "Smithy" to the children, dug them out of the kitchen to admire it.

"Mrs Cornelius will want to know that you've seen it."

"It's a very neat tree," said Jane.

Benita looked up at the shining new decorations.

"It seems as if it felt embarrassed here."

Alan was looking at the parcels under the tree.

"Smithy, how will Grandmother Cornelius know which is for which?" he asked. "There's no labels."

"They've left a chart, dear," Miss Smith explained. "Blue paper for men. Green for women. Red for boys. Yellow for girls."

Jane started to move back towards the kitchen. "Just like a Santa does in a shop."

It was that night that the first grown-up dared to break out from the drawing-room. It was old Hans Cornelius; he was not playing in the rubber of bridge which was going on, so he slipped quietly out of the room, and, like a homing pigeon, found his way through the green baize door. The Chrystals, Alan, Benita and Gardiner were having Welsh rarebit for supper, and while they ate it Ted was describing a night when the curtain had stuck and would not come down at the end of *Dick Whittington*.

"And there was Miss Dolores Dear, always one to be upset easily, stepping forward and saying:

And now we've had enough of this and that,

Let's say farewell to Whittington . . .

and that was where I had to come forward for the 'and cat,' but the curtain stuck, so she starts again and . . ."

Old Hans had come in so quietly that at first they did not see him standing in the doorway. Then he said, "That Welsh rarebit smells very good, Mrs Chrystal. Could I have a bit?"

Old Hans told Jan where he had been, and Jan told Anna, and Anna told Lalla, and Lalla told Virginia, who, of course, passed on the news to Tom. So the next day, which was Christmas Eve, there was great rivalry amongst the grown-ups to cut out of the bridge rubbers, for it was so lovely and Christmassy in the kitchen, with paper rings festooned across the ceiling and a gay little tree in the window.

"And to-night we're going to light it," said Rinke.

"And leave the curtains open," Jane explained.

"Rosa says it's to show Jesus the way to come," Gardiner added.

"If you can get out of playing bridge, Mummy," Benita implored, "do come here after dinner, for that's when we shall sing carols."

"The kids," Alan explained, nodding at Peter, Jane and Rinke, "are coming down in their dressing-gowns."

"I'll be there somehow," Virginia promised.

"I wouldn't miss it," said old Hans.

"Nor us," Jan and Anna agreed.

"Count on me," Tom stated firmly.

"What about you?" Gardiner asked his mother.

"I'll be there," said Lalla.

So that evening, after dinner, on one excuse and another, everybody slipped out of the drawing-room and away to the kitchen, until Mrs Cornelius, with the cards in front of her, had no one with whom to play bridge. She rang the bell for Miss Smith, but Miss Smith, enraptured, was in the kitchen and did not hear it. Furiously Mrs Cornelius rang again, and again nobody came. So, determined to tell everybody what she thought of them, she left the drawing-room and marched out into the great hall. She might, and very nearly did, miss opening the green baize door, but something guided her to it.

Standing unseen, looking into the kitchen, Mrs Cornelius forgot the angry things she had meant to say. In the window was the little tree, nothing like so grand as the one in the hall, but gay with lights. All round it stood her family, with Miss Smith and the Chrystals. They were singing "Good King Wenceslas," old Hans' voice booming as the king.

> *Bring me flesh and bring me wine,*
> *Bring me pine-logs hither;*
> *Thou and I will see him dine,*
> *When we bear them thither.*

Everybody sang the next lines, and then Gardiner's shrill treble rang out:

> *Sire, the night is darker now,*
> *And the wind blows stronger,*

Fails my heart, I know not how
I can go no longer.

It was as if Mrs Cornelius's heart had been made of ice, and now suddenly the ice was melting. She was not cross, she was envious. She wanted more than she had wanted anything for years to feel she could join that party round the tree, and not by her mere presence spoil the beauty of the evening for everybody else. She meant to go back to the drawing-room, and would have gone, but as she moved, a board creaked and, just as Mrs Cornelius had feared, the carol-singing faltered. But Rosa and Ted were not having that.

"Madam!" Rosa said, making room for her.

"Come on, Madam," Ted added.

Mrs Cornelius came on and found herself singing words she had forgotten she had ever known.

Therefore, Christian men, be sure,
Wealth or rank possessing,
Ye who now will bless the poor,
Shall yourselves find blessing.

THE STORY OF BROTHER JOHANNICK
AND HIS SILVER BELL

retold by Elizabeth Clark

This is a very old story — an ancient legend of Christmas-time — from Brittany, where it has been told and told again for many hundreds of years. It is the story of Brother Johannick and his silver bell.

It was long ago — five hundred years, or perhaps six hundred — that Brother Johannick lived, all alone on the tiny Isle Notre-Dame that lay midway in the wide estuary of the river Rance. At the mouth of the river is the port of St. Malo. Inland were great forests, and there, all the year round, wood-cutters were busy; and cargoes of logs and faggots of wood were carried down the river to keep the fires burning that warmed the houses and cooked the food of the folk of St. Malo. The logs were loaded on large heavy boats called gabares — the men who worked the boats were called gabariers. Up and down the river they sailed all through the year from the little town of Pludihen to the great port of St. Malo.

It was in winter-time that the gabariers were most busy. Many loads of logs and many bundles of faggots were needed then to keep the hearths of St. Malo burning. And it was in winter-time also that the boatmen were most grateful to Brother Johannick and his silver bell. For when days grew cold and nights were long the sea fogs came rolling in from the Channel, spreading far and wide over the marshes so that no river banks, no houses, no landmarks could be seen. Then

the wide mouth of the Rance was a dangerous place. There were strong tides and currents; there were sand-bars and mud-banks and little rocky islands. And in the thick grey fog no man could tell where his boat might be drifting unless there was something to steer by.

It was on those dark nights and days of cold, thick fog that Brother Johannick did his work. All night and all day while the fog lasted he stood by the shore of Isle Notre-Dame and rang his silver bell. The clear ringing sound floated out across the water and gabariers would listen and say: "Ah! there I hear Brother Johannick's bell. Steer a little farther to the right. I can tell by the sound that we are too near the shore." Or: "Listen – there is the bell. We are drawing near Isle Notre-Dame – be careful of the current, there is a rock hereabouts." And they blessed Brother Johannick for his goodness and his care.

They did what they could to show they were grateful to him. On clear days and nights as the gabares passed the island, the boatmen would drop a big log or a good faggot of wood overboard just where the current would carry it safely and surely to the shore of Isle Notre-Dame. Brother Johannick thankfully dragged the wood to land and piled it by his shelter, and in his turn he blessed the gabariers for their warm hearts and kind thought for him.

The years went by and Brother Johannick grew old. His long white beard hung down over his brown robe. His back was bent and he went slowly. It was not so easy for him to wade into deep water and to pull in heavy logs and faggots. So the pile of wood by his shelter was smaller and his fire was not so warm nor so comforting. But his heart was brave, and still day by day and night by night, when storms came and darkness and thick sea fogs, Brother Johannick never failed to ring his silver bell.

Then there came a year when it turned bitterly cold just a week before Christmas. There was hard frost each night; the stones of the island were white with it, and where the little spring trickled down, great icicles hung from the rocks. With the frost came a thick white fog. It never lifted; day after day it covered the marshes, the river and the island. And by day and by night, Brother Johannick rang his silver bell.

Christmas Eve came. His fire had gone out. He had no more logs. His old brown robe was thin and ragged and damp with mist. He was shivering and very weary. But he sang Christmas hymns as he rang his bell and his heart was warm with joy and gratefulness as he thought of Christmas Day to come and the message of love to all men.

The hours of the night went by and presently he stopped his ringing. "Midnight is surely passed," he said. "I must kneel a moment to say a prayer, for Christmas Day is here. "And he knelt down upon the shore to say "Our Father." He could scarcely kneel, he was so weary and so stiff with cold; and when he came to the end of his prayer his voice was only a whisper and he did not rise from his knees. His tired old head nodded forward; Brother Johannick gave a little sigh and slipped down and lay fast asleep beside the ashes of his fire.

In the little town of Pludihen on the Rance, the fog was thick too that Christmas Eve. But the houses were warm. Every hearth had its great Christmas log; there was plenty of wood in the forests for all.

Père Suliac the gabarier sat warming himself by the blaze. He was very comfortable and his wife was cooking something that smelled very good in the pot that hung over the fire.

But Père Suliac was not quite happy in his mind. He fidgeted, and every now and then he went to the window and opened the wooden shutter and looked out into the fog and listened. "I am thinking of Brother Johannick," he said when his wife asked what troubled him. "He must be cold on that island of his, and I am wondering what he is doing about a fire. With this fog he will not manage to find many logs floating in the water. I have a good mind," said Père Suliac suddenly, "to take him some wood this very night, to give him a fire for Christmas. He does enough for us out there in the dark and the cold; one should do something for him."

But Mère Suliac was frightened. "Why should you go out so

34

late on such a night?" she said crossly. "Brother Johannick stays on the island of his own free will. Nobody makes him do it. Stay and be warm by your fire this Christmas Eve."

Père Suliac said no more, but he thought to himself: "The holy man shall have a log for Christmas, all the same."

Very late that night – it was past midnight – Père Suliac sat up in his bed and listened for the silver bell. Mère Suliac lay fast asleep, but he had only closed his eyes and pretended he was sleeping. He had a plan to carry out as soon as all was quiet in the house.

"There is no sound of the bell," he said to himself. "What can have happened? It was ringing well enough a while ago."

He listened again. "No – there it is after all, and how strong and clear it sounds. Surely the good God gives strength to the holy man's arms!"

He slipped quietly out of bed in the dark and felt about for his clothes. But they were not there! Then he laughed a little to himself. "The good wife has hidden my clothes while my eyes were shut," he said. "She guessed what I meant to do and she thought she would stop me. But there is the old sheepskin coat hanging by the door and that will do well enough. There is no one to see that I am only half dressed, in this fog, and the holy man will not mind!"

He belted the old coat round him and slipped out barefoot down to the river where his boat was moored; there was a good pile of logs and some faggots on board. He hoisted his sails; there was just a breath of wind, and with the current it would carry him straight to Isle Notre-Dame. And it was easy to steer, in spite of fog and darkness, for never had he heard the bell ring so sweet and clear.

But it was not only the bell that guided him; a light was shining through the mist. Père Suliac looked and looked again. "One would say there was moonlight somewhere," he said. "But there is no moon tonight."

Presently he saw that the light must come from Isle Notre-Dame. It was not a red glow such as a fire would give; it shone silver bright. The fog was turned to a shining mist and from the mist the bell rang sweet and clear.

Père Suliac was puzzled and almost afraid. "This is the time of Christmas," he said, "when angels sing songs upon earth and surely this is a heavenly light. Perhaps the angels themselves are upon Isle Notre-Dame." And then he remembered that he was wearing nothing but the old sheepskin coat. He was troubled as he thought of it.

"Certainly," said Père Suliac, "it is not suitable or respectable that I should come before the angels dressed like this." And with his knife he slit a long strip from his mainsail and wrapped it round himself under his coat like a kind of kilt and tied it with a piece of cord.

"There!" he said, looking at himself with satisfaction. "Now I am more properly clothed."

And then, suddenly, the boat came out of the mist into a little clear space of water. In the midst was Isle Notre-Dame; all round the fog lay like a shining wall but overhead the stars were clear. The light came from the island – a soft clear shining light, so that Père Suliac could see Brother Johannick, very old and weary, lying fast asleep upon the cold white frosty ground by the ashes of a burned-out fire. But beside Brother Johannick there stood a little Child all in white, and in his hand the Child held the silver bell, ringing it steadily and sweetly so that the sound floated far across the river and the wide marshlands beyond.

The boat drifted gently on the bright water, and when it came near the shore the Child put out a little hand and beckoned. Père Suliac made the boat fast and waded to the shore with a great log and an armful of faggots. Then he knelt down and laid the wood at the feet of the little child and bowed his head. And the Child smiled and laid a hand on Père Suliac's head and then on the wood, blessing both.

It seemed to Père Suliac then that all the Isle Notre-Dame was full of the songs of angels with a wonderful feeling of loving-kindness and of joy all around; and in his mind he said: "This is no angel; this is the heavenly Child." And a light sprang up so clear and dazzling that he closed his eyes.

When he looked again the light had gone. There was only

the bare little island sparkling with frost in the starlight. But the night was clear and on the cold black ashes of Brother Johannick's fire, where he had laid the wood, bright flames were darting and crackling. The Christmas log was alight and blazing; and beside the fire Brother Johannick was awaking and the silver bell was in his hand.

Père Suliac told him all that he had seen; and Brother Johannick said: "Most surely it was the heavenly Child." And they knelt down together to give thanks for Christmas Day and for all the love that is put in men's hearts.

Then Père Suliac landed his load of wood and when morning came he sailed back in the sunshine across the water to Pludihen.

Some of the men by the waterside laughed when they saw Père Suliac so oddly dressed in his sheepskin coat and his sailcloth kilt. But they did not laugh when they heard his story. They were glad and grateful to Brother Johannick for all his patient watchfulness, to Père Suliac for his kindness, and most of all they gave thanks to our Father in Heaven for the love he sends to the hearts of all men.

And the old story tells them that henceforward the gabariers of Pludihen dressed themselves as Père Suliac was dressed that Christmas Eve, in coat and sailcloth kilt, that they might keep in memory all that had happened on that most wonderful night.

THE CHRISTMAS ROSE

A Scandinavian tale
retold by Stephen Corrin

Long long ago, in the dim and distant past, deep in the Great Forest in ice-cold north Norway, there lived a man and his wife and their five children. The father had been unjustly accused of robbery and was forced to live the life of an outlaw in a cave far from the nearest village. The only food the family had was the wild berries which the children gathered and the animals which their father occasionally managed to hunt down. Their mother's time was spent picking ferns to serve as bedding and collecting wood for the fire. Living like this, they all looked so wild and dirty that if ever they ventured into the village people would immediately lock their doors. Nobody ever even said good morning to them, let alone smiled, but sometimes – though this was extremely rare – they would find a bundle of old clothing or a packet of left-over food on a door-step.

One summer afternoon when the mother was trudging back from the village to her cave-home, lugging her old sack of throwaways behind her, she passed the monastery. A small door had been left open and through it she caught a glimpse of a beautiful garden. The powerful scent of the honeysuckle and roses tempted her inside, so she put down her sack to walk around and admire all the multi-coloured blooms.

Suddenly she was startled by a threatening shout. "What are you doing there, woman! Be off with you! This is the

private property of the Abbot, no women are allowed in here. Away with you!" It was the monastery gardener.

But the woman was not easily scared. "I'm doing no harm," she retorted. "I'll go in my own good time."

"You'll go now or I'll throw you out," bawled the gardener.

"Just you come and try," she laughed, looking down at his small figure. He called three monks to help him, but the woman was too much for them, and her loud screams and curses eventually brought out the Abbot himself.

"Let *me* deal with this woman," he said. "Now, my good lady, what is it you want? Would you, perhaps, like to pick some of my flowers?"

"No, I would not," replied the woman firmly. "Our own garden in the Great Forest at Christmas-time is much more beautiful than this one." Now the Abbot knew that his garden was the finest in the land, so he simply smiled good-naturedly.

"You may smile, Lord Abbot," said the woman, "but over Christmas, right outside our own cave-home, the Great Forest becomes a magnificent garden in honour of the Miracle Birth. Flowers of every season suddenly spring up. And there are special Christmas Roses too which have silver petals and golden stamens."

The Abbot scratched his brow. Childhood memories came back to him of stories about a wondrous garden in the Great Forest.

"I should like very much to see your garden," he said after a long pause. "Will you come and guide me there next Yuletide?"

"Will you first promise not to drive us out of our cave-home?" asked the woman.

"I most certainly would never drive a family out of its home," said the Abbot emphatically. "On the contrary, if your claim is true, I will ask the Lord Bishop to grant your husband a pardon. Then he would no longer be an outlaw and you could come and live in the village."

The woman could not hide her pleasure and amazement. "Thank you, Lord Abbot," she murmured. "Next Christmas

Eve my eldest son will come and fetch you and lead you to our cave-home. Please wait for him by the great oak tree and please do not bring anyone with you except your gardener."

The Abbot was somewhat surprised at this condition, but he agreed. He gave her his blessing, and she picked up her sack and started her journey back home.

When the Bishop heard from the Abbot the story of the Christmas Garden in the Great Forest he started wondering about the robber whom he had made an outlaw. "Surely," he thought, "if such a miracle can take place outside the cave-home of the robber family there must be some good in the head of that family." He pondered deeply on this and told the Abbot that if the story of the miracle garden did indeed prove to be true, he would grant the outlaw a pardon. In that way, thought the Bishop, perhaps his five children will grow up into peaceful citizens instead of becoming a gang of robbers. "I look forward to seeing those miraculous roses of silver and gold," he concluded.

At last Christmas Eve came round again and the Abbot, accompanied by his gardener, set out for the Forest in the direction of the great oak tree. Sure enough the eldest son was waiting for them there, exactly as his mother had arranged. The gardener kept grumbling under his breath about it all being a lot of nonsense and how he wished he were sitting at home by his fireside, watching his wife busying herself with the goose and the Christmas decorations. Complaining all the time, he followed the Abbot and the boy until they arrived at the opening to a cave. They had to bend double to get inside and there, by a log fire, sat the mother, while her children were spread all over the floor, playing with their 'toys' – bits of stick and stones. Further in the father himself lay sprawled on an old torn mattress which consisted mainly of straw stuffing.

"I haven't seen any sign of your miracle silver flowers," the gardener burst out.

"Silence!" commanded the Abbot.

"Pray sit by the fire and rest yourselves," said the woman.

41

"If you fall asleep I'll wake you when the hour has come for you to see what I have described to you." Abbot and gardener dozed by the fire, weary after their long journey, but they were soon awakened by the chimes of Christmas bells. The whole family hurried to the cave opening, followed by their two visitors.

"How remarkable to be able to hear the church bells so far away, here in the Great Forest," said the Abbot. But the Great Forest looked as dark and forbidding as ever and the grumpy gardener made no effort to hide his opinion of it. Then, with startling suddenness, the chiming of the bells stopped and the all-pervading blackness changed to a rosy dawn. The snow melted rapidly, revealing healthy green shoots. The Forest floor became overspread with multi-coloured spring flowers and right in the midst, as though enthroned, gleamed a host of Christmas Roses, with silver petals and golden stamens. The air was alive with bees, butterflies and birds. But even more than the silver and gold of the roses, what astonished the Abbot was the family itself. Father, mother and five children were completely changed. Their faces were filled with happiness and pride, and their eyes shone with a heavenly glow. Overcome with joy at this miracle, the Abbot knelt down and murmured a prayer of praise.

But the effect on the gardener was utterly different.

"Witchcraft!" he cried. "Devilry! The hand of Satan!"

At these words the rosy dawn faded and blackness spread like an icy wind over the Great Forest. As the family ran shivering into the cave the garden disappeared, and the Abbot and his gardener fled away, clutching each other for fear of falling, for they could not see in the pitch darkness. Once, indeed, the Abbot fell on to the frozen earth, but the gardener hauled him up and dragged him desperately on in the direction of the monastery.

When they finally reached it, the Abbot was so exhausted that he had to be put to bed, where he fell into what appeared to be a deep sleep, a radiant smile on his face. But, alas, he was never to wake again; he died in his sleep. Then one of the monks noticed that he was clutching something in his right hand. It was the root of a plant; he must have pulled it up when he tripped.

The gardener was told to plant the root in the Abbot's garden and this he did. Spring, summer and autumn passed, and although a few green leaves appeared, there were no signs of any flowers. Then winter came and the ground was carpeted with snow. And it was on Christmas morning itself that flowers appeared – silver petals encircling stamens of gold. They were Christmas Roses!

"These are the very same that I saw in the robber's garden," thought the gardener, and he immediately plucked three of these miracle flowers and took them to the Bishop.

"The Abbot has kept his promise to you, my Lord Bishop," he said. "The robber did indeed have a miracle garden, for these flowers are the very same as we saw there, and they grew from the root which my master, the Lord Abbot, held tight in his hand on his death-bed."

The Bishop was much moved and he made out a pardon for the outlaw, signed and sealed it, and had the gardener deliver it.

However, when the gardener reached the cave-home, he found the entrance blocked, and when the outlaw caught sight of him he threatened to give him the thrashing of his life.

"It is all your fault that we have no Christmas garden," he shouted.

"Yes, I know that," said the gardener humbly. "I just could not believe in such a miracle. My faith was not great enough."

"Go away and leave us in peace," said the outlaw.

"I will, I will," said the gardener in a pleading voice, "but first let me hand you the pardon from my Lord Bishop. You are no longer an outlaw and you are free to come and live in the village with the rest of us. Indeed, you will be made most welcome, you and your family."

And so they left their cave-home in the Great Forest and began a new life in the village with their old friends.

THE REAL TRUE
FATHER CHRISTMAS

Roy Fuller

One December a little girl went shopping with her mother in a large department store. In the toy department a sort of cave had been constructed. On the outside of it there was a notice saying "FATHER CHRISTMAS'S GROTTO" and giving the price of admission. The main inducement to enter was the promise that every visitor would receive a gift from Father Christmas.

"Do you want to visit Father Christmas's Grotto?" asked the little girl's mother.

"Not particularly," said the little girl.

"Well, I think you'd better," said the mother. "I've a few things to buy I don't want you to see. When you've finished inside, go to that stall where they were demonstrating atomic submarines and I'll join you there."

The mother paid the price of admission and the little girl entered the grotto. Her reluctance to do so in the first place was not because she was blasé; rather that she felt it would be embarrassing to meet a fraud – a dressed-up man masquerading as Father Christmas. He would be putting on an act and she would have to put on an act as well; in other words, pretend that she thought he really was Father Christmas.

It was not even as though she believed that somewhere there was a true Father Christmas who the man in the grotto was pretending to be; she knew very well – she had known for two or three years – that Father Christmas was an inven-

44

tion of parents to give their children pleasure at Christmas time. Moreover, her mother knew that she knew, so being sent out of the way via the grotto was somehow a rather humiliating way of being sent out of the way – as though she were still aged about four.

Also, she was the only patron going into the grotto, and that made her self-conscious. Perhaps at this time of day there were fewer people in the department or the admission to the grotto was priced too high or its reputation had become notorious – rotten presents, say, or a feeble Father Christmas whose beard didn't fit properly.

The entrance to the grotto was both deserted and gloomy. For some reason a battered effigy of Mickey Mouse stood against one of the canvas walls; no doubt it was disinterred from the store's cellars for any occasion in which children were involved. A hidden loudspeaker of poor quality was playing Christmas carols. The canvas walls made a right-angled turn leading to a small, still quite gloomy open space where a figure in red robes sat in a sleigh, also of battered aspect. Some greyish icicles hung from the ceiling. What a grotty grotto, thought the little girl.

"Come along, my dear," said the red-robed figure through his white beard and moustache. "Don't be shy."

There were no other visitors in this inner sanctum either. There was a little stool by the sleigh, to which the Father Christmas figure pointed his red sleeve (from which an ordinary shirt cuff protruded).

"Sit down here, there's a good girl,' he said. 'Now, what's your name, my angel?"

"Arabella Tomkins."

"What a lovely name!" said Father Christmas.

"Do you think so?"

"I certainly do."

"I think it's a silly name," said Arabella.

"Good gracious, you mustn't say that," exclaimed Father Christmas.

"Why not?"

"Well it's your name, isn't it? You've got to go through life with it and—'

"Not if I marry," said Arabella.

"No, I see that."

"Not that that would be much help, since Arabella's the sillier part."

"Oh that's what you think, is it?"

"Don't you?"

"I'm not here to think," said Father Christmas. "I'm here to get on rapidly with my job, which is to ask you what you want me to bring you for Christmas and also to give you a gift out of this 'ere bag."

"Why do you say 'This 'ere bag' in that different voice?"

"Because I'm a humorous fellow," said Father Christmas. "Come on now, Arabella Tomkins, let's get it over with. What shall I drop down your chimney on the twenty-fourth? Doll, doll's cradle, toy trombone?"

"I think we could skip all that and get on right away with the gift part of your job," said Arabella. "You see I know you couldn't be Father Christmas, even if Father Christmas really existed."

"I say, you pitch it a bit strong, don't you?"

"Well, what I say is true, isn't it?"

Father Christmas didn't speak for a full ten seconds. Then slowly he said: "No, it is not. What *is* true is that up and down the country and all over the world at this time of year there are a lot of people dressed up as Father Christmas. On Christmas Eve the number probably goes up. The supply is regulated by the demand in accordance with economic law. Obviously I couldn't be here and also at Selfridges. But that doesn't mean that somewhere there isn't a real, true Father Christmas. Do you follow me?"

"Yes," said Arabella, "but—"

"On Christmas Eve," continued Father Christmas, "the part of Father Christmas is usually played by the father of the family. Father Christmases in the street – selling cheap mechanical toys, say, or advertising restaurants' Christmas

dinners − are ordinary street-traders or sandwich-board men just dressed up for the seasonal occasion. Father Christmases in the better stores − I'm sure the one at Selfridges, for instance − are, more likely than not, unemployed actors, a very talented and respectable class of men. But among all those Father Christmases is the one veritable, old, original Father Christmas."

"And do you mean to say," said Arabella in sarcastic tones, "that he rides on a sleigh and is pulled by reindeer and—"

"Yes I do, and he does."

Arabella laughed.

"What is more," said Father Christmas, extremely seriously, "I am him. Or should it be 'I am he'? Anyway, I am the real Father Christmas. You may go on sniggering, Arabella, but that can't affect the truth of the matter, which is that by a strange chance − one which may never occur again − you have met the one right, regular Father Christmas out of thousands of necessary imitations. Feel my hands."

Arabella did so.

"You see," said Father Christmas. "They're cold; cold as the Prussian plains I come from. You think my whiskers are false, don't you? Pull them."

Arabella reached out and pulled the white beard. Father Christmas uttered a slight 'ouch' and the beard remained fast.

"One final proof of my identity, if further proof were needed. I know without your telling me what you would most dearly like for Christmas, Arabella Tomkins, and I hereby solemnly promise to bring it to you. When you open the parcel on Christmas morning and find your heart's desire, remember this one moment and me, the old, original Father Christmas, who (or should it be 'whom'?) you once doubted."

Father Christmas's tones had become quite deep and tragic, and he put a bent forefinger quickly to each eye in turn, probably to dam back a starting tear.

Then he said: "I think I hear someone else coming along. Up you get, Arabella, and on your way. Here is your some-what miserable interim present."

He fished about in the sack at his feet and brought out an oblong package wrapped in purple tissue paper. "This is not my choice, of course – and I'm sure it wouldn't be yours. It's just one of the limited selection provided by the management as advertised at the entrance and included in the price of admission to this 'ere grotto. Goodbye. Happy Christmas."

"Happy Christmas," said Arabella faintly, rather overcome by Father Christmas's eloquence. She walked out of the grotto. Just before the exit stood a down-at-heel represent-ation of Donald Duck.

Arabella said nothing to her mother about her conversation with Father Christmas. The purple tissue-wrapped package proved to be the game of snakes and ladders, two versions of which she already possessed. But she had not previously possessed the main present she found in her pillowslip on her bed on Christmas morning – and which was indeed, as Father Christmas had prophesied, the thing she wanted most. How had he done it? The fact that he had done it, thought Arabella, did not make him the real Father Christmas, however, any more than a conjuror's production of a rabbit makes him a real magician.

A CHRISTMAS CAROL

Charles Dickens

Old Marley was dead, dead as a doornail. Did Scrooge know he was dead? Of course he did. How could it be otherwise? Scrooge was his sole administrator, his sole friend and sole mourner. Scrooge was not dreadfully cut up by the sad event; he was an excellent man of business and on the very day of the funeral he solemnised it with an undoubted bargain.

Scrooge never painted out Old Marley's name. There it stood, years afterwards, above the warehouse door: Scrooge and Marley. The firm was known as Scrooge and Marley. Sometimes, people new to the business called Scrooge Scrooge and sometimes Marley, but he answered to both names. It was all the same to him.

Oh! But he was a tight-fisted hand at the grindstone, Scrooge! a squeezing, wrenching, grasping, scraping, clutching, covetous old sinner! Hard and sharp as flint, from which no steel had ever struck out generous fire; secret, and self-contained, and solitary as an oyster. The cold within him froze his old features, nipped his pointed nose, shrivelled his cheek, stiffened his gait; made his eyes red, his thin lips blue; and spoke out shrewdly in his grating voice.

Nobody ever stopped him in the street to say, "My dear Scrooge, how are you? When will you come to see me?" No beggars implored him to bestow a trifle, no children asked him what o'clock it was, no man or woman ever once in all his life inquired of Scrooge the way to such and such a place. Even the blind men's dogs appeared to know him; and when they saw him coming, would tug their owners into doorways.

But what did Scrooge care! It was the very thing he liked. Once upon a time, on Christmas Eve, old Scrooge sat busy in his counting-house. It was cold, bleak, biting, foggy weather and he could hear the people outside go wheezing past, beating their breasts and stamping their feet upon the pavement stones to warm them.

The door of Scrooge's counting-house was open that he might keep his eye upon his clerk, who, in a dismal little cell beyond, a sort of tank, was copying letters. Scrooge had a very small fire, but the clerk's fire was so very much smaller that it looked like one coal. But he couldn't replenish it, for Scrooge kept the coal-box in his own room.

"A Merry Christmas, uncle! God save you!" cried a cheerful voice. It was the voice of Scrooge's nephew, who came upon him so quickly that this was the first intimation he had of his approach.

"Bah!" said Scrooge. "Humbug!"

He had so heated himself with rapid walking in the fog and frost, this nephew of Scrooge's, that he was all in a glow; his face was ruddy and handsome; his eyes sparkled and his breath smoked again.

"Christmas a humbug, uncle!" said Scrooge's nephew. "You don't mean that, I am sure?"

"I do," said Scrooge. "Merry Christmas! What right have you to be merry? What reason have you to be merry? You're poor enough."

"Come, then," returned the nephew gaily. "What right have you to be dismal? What reason have you to be morose? You're rich enough."

Scrooge, having no better answer ready on the spur of the moment, said, "Bah!" again; and followed it up with "Humbug."

"Don't be cross, uncle!" said the nephew.

"What else can I be," returned the uncle, "when I live in

such a world of fools as this? Merry Christmas! Out upon Merry Christmas! What's Christmas time to you but a time for paying bills without money? If I could work my will, every idiot who goes about with 'Merry Christmas' on his lips should be boiled in his own pudding and buried with a stake of holly through his heart!"

"Uncle!" pleaded the nephew.

"Nephew!" returned the uncle sternly, "keep Christmas in your own way, and let me keep it in mine."

"But you don't keep it!" said the nephew.

"Let me leave it alone then," said Scrooge.

"I have always thought of Christmas time as a good time," replied the nephew, "a kind, forgiving, charitable, pleasant time, and though, uncle, it has never put a scrap of gold in my pocket, I believe it *has* done me good and *will* do me good; and I say, God bless it!"

The clerk in the tank involuntarily applauded. Becoming immediately sensible of the impropriety, he poked the fire and extinguished the last spark for ever.

"Let me hear another word from *you*," said Scrooge, "and you'll keep *your* Christmas by losing your situation!"

"Don't be angry, uncle. Come! Dine with us tomorrow."

Scrooge said that he would see him − . Yes, indeed he did. He went the whole length of the expression and said he would see him in that extremity first.

"But why?" cried Scrooge's nephew. "Why?"

"Why did you get married?" said Scrooge.

"Because I fell in love."

"Because you fell in love!" growled Scrooge. "Good afternoon!"

"But, uncle, you never came to see me before that happened. Why give it as a reason for not coming now?"

"Good afternoon," repeated Scrooge.

"I want nothing from you; I ask nothing of you; why can't we be friends?"

"Good afternoon," said Scrooge.

"I am sorry with all my heart to find you so resolute," said the nephew. "We have never had any quarrel and I'll keep my Christmas humour to the last! So A Merry Christmas, uncle!"

"Good afternoon!" said Scrooge.

"And A Happy New Year!"

"Good afternoon," said Scrooge.

His nephew left the room without an angry word. He stopped at the outer door to bestow the greetings of the season on the clerk, who, cold as he was, was warmer than Scrooge, for he returned the greetings cordially.

"There's another fellow," muttered Scrooge, who over-heard him; "my clerk, with fifteen shillings a week and a wife and family, talking about a merry Christmas!"

In letting Scrooge's nephew out the clerk had let two other people in. They were pleasant gentlemen and they now stood before Scrooge with books and papers in their hands and bowed to him.

"Scrooge and Marley's, I believe," said one of the gentlemen, looking at his list. "Have I the pleasure of addressing Mr. Scrooge or Mr. Marley?"

"Mr. Marley has been dead these seven years," Scrooge replied. "Seven years ago this very night."

"We have no doubt his liberality is well represented by his surviving partner," said the gentleman.

It certainly was, for they had been kindred spirits. At the ominous word "Liberality" Scrooge frowned and shook his head.

"At this festive season of the year, Mr. Scrooge," said the gentleman, "it is more than usually desirable that we should make some slight provision for the poor and destitute, who suffer greatly at the present time. Many thousands are in want of common necessaries; hundreds of thousands are in want of common comforts, sir."

"Are there no prisons?" asked Scrooge.

"Plenty of prisons," said the gentleman.

"And the union workhouses?" demanded Scrooge. "Are they still in operation?"

"They are. Still," returned the gentleman. "I wish I could say they were not."

"The treadmill and the Poor Law are in full vigour, then?" said Scrooge.

"Both very busy, sir."

"Oh! I was afraid from what you first said that something had occurred to stop them in their useful course," said Scrooge. "I'm very glad to hear it."

"Under the impression that they scarcely furnish Christmas cheer of mind or body to the multitude," returned the gentleman, "a few of us are endeavouring to raise a fund to buy the poor some meat and drink and means of warmth. What shall I put you down for?"

"Nothing!" Scrooge replied.

"You wish to be anonymous?"

"I wish to be left alone," said Scrooge. "I don't make merry myself at Christmas and I can't afford to make idle people merry. I help to support the establishments I have mentioned – they cost enough; and those who are badly off must go there."

"Many can't go there; and many would rather die."

"If they would rather die," said Scrooge, "they had better do it, and decrease the surplus population. Good afternoon, gentlemen!"

Seeing clearly it would be useless to pursue the point, the gentlemen withdrew.

At length the hour of shutting up the counting-house arrived. With an ill-will Scrooge dismounted from his stool and tacitly admitted the fact to the expectant clerk in the tank, who instantly snuffed his candle out, and put on his hat.

"You'll want all day to-morrow, I suppose?" said Scrooge.

"If it's convenient, sir."

"It's not convenient," said Scrooge, "and it's not fair. If I was to stop half a crown for it, you'd think yourself ill-used, I'll be bound?"

The clerk smiled faintly.

"And yet," said Scrooge, "you don't think *me* ill-used, when I pay a day's wages for no work."

The clerk observed that it was only once a year.

"A poor excuse for picking a man's pocket every twenty-fifth of December!" said Scrooge, buttoning his greatcoat to the chin. "But I suppose you must have the whole day. Be here all the earlier next morning."

The clerk promised that he would and Scrooge walked out with a growl. The office was closed in a twinkling and the clerk, with the long ends of his white comforter dangling below his waist (for he boasted no greatcoat) went down a slide on Cornhill, at the end of a lane of boys, in honour of its being Christmas Eve, and then ran home to Camden Town as hard as he could pelt, to play at blindman's-buff.

Scrooge took his melancholy dinner in his usual melancholy tavern; and having read all the newspapers, and beguiled the rest of the evening with his banker's book, went home to bed. He lived in a gloomy suite of rooms which had once belonged to his deceased partner. It was part of a lowering pile of buildings in a yard which was so dark that even Scrooge, who knew its every stone, had to grope with his hands.

Now it is a fact that there was nothing at all particular about the knocker on the door except that it was very large. It is also a fact that Scrooge had seen it, night and morning, during his whole residence in that place; also that Scrooge had as little of what is called fancy about him as any man in the city of London. And then let any man explain to me, if he can, how it happened that Scrooge, having his key in the lock of the door, saw in the knocker, without its undergoing any intermediate process of change – not a knocker but Marley's face.

Marley's face. It was not in impenetrable shadow as the other objects in the yard were, but had a dismal light about it, like a bad lobster in a dark cellar. It was not angry or ferocious but looked at Scrooge as Marley used to look, with ghostly spectacles turned up on its ghostly forehead. The hair was curiously stirred, as if by breath or hot air; and though the eyes were wide open, they were perfectly motionless. That, and its livid colour, made it horrible; but its horror seemed to be in spite of the face and beyond its control, rather than a part of its own expression.

As Scrooge looked fixedly at this phenomenon, it was a knocker again.

To say that he was not startled, or that his blood was not conscious of a terrible sensation to which it had been a stranger from infancy, would be untrue. But he put his hand upon the key he had relinquished, turned it sturdily, walked in, and lighted his candle.

He *did* pause, with a moment's irresolution, before he shut the door; and he *did* look cautiously behind it first, as if he half expected to be terrified with the sight of Marley's pigtail sticking out into the hall. But there was nothing on the back of the door except the screws and nuts that held the knocker on, so he said, "Pooh, pooh!" and closed the door with a bang.

The sound resounded through the house like thunder. But Scrooge was not a man to be frightened by echoes. He fastened the door, and walked across the hall and up the stairs, slowly too; trimming his candle as he went.

He closed his door and locked himself in – double-locked himself in, which was not his custom. Thus secured against surprise, he took off his cravat; put on his dressing gown and slippers, and his nightcap, and sat down before the fire to take his gruel.

As he threw his head back in the chair his glance happened to rest upon a bell, a disused bell, that hung in the room, and communicated, for some purpose now forgotten, with a room in the highest story in the building. It was with great astonishment, and with a strange, inexplicable dread, that as he looked he saw this bell begin to swing. It swung so softly that it scarcely made a sound; but soon it rang out loudly, and so did every bell in the house.

This might have lasted half a minute, or a minute, but it seemed an hour. The bells ceased as they had begun, together. They were succeeded by a clanking noise, deep down below; as if some person were dragging a heavy chain over the casks in the wine-merchant's cellar. Scrooge then remembered to have heard that ghosts in haunted houses were described as dragging chains.

The cellar door flew open with a booming sound, and then he heard the noise much louder, on the floors below; then coming up the stairs; then coming straight towards his door.

"It's humbug still!" said Scrooge, "I won't believe it."

His colour changed, though, when, without a pause, it came on through the heavy door, and passed into the room before his eyes. Upon its coming in, the dying flame leaped up, as though it cried, "I know him! Marley's ghost!" and fell again.

The same face; the very same. Marley in his pigtail, usual waistcoat, tights and boots; the tassels on the latter bristling, like his pigtail, and his coat-skirts, and the hair upon his head. The chain he drew was clasped about his middle. It was long, and wound about him like a tail; and it was made (Scrooge observed it closely) of cash-boxes, keys, padlocks, ledgers, deeds, and heavy purses wrought in steel. His body was transparent; so that Scrooge, observing him, and looking through his waistcoat, could see the two buttons on his coat behind.

"How now!" said Scrooge, caustic and cold as ever. "What do you want with me?"

"Much!" – Marley's voice, no doubt about it.

"Who are you?"

"Ask me who I *was*."

"Who *were* you then?" said Scrooge, raising his voice.

"In life I was your partner, Jacob Marley."

"Can you – can you sit down?" asked Scrooge, looking doubtfully at him.

"I can."

"Do it, then."

Scrooge asked the question because he didn't know whether a ghost so transparent might find himself in a condition to take a chair; and felt that in the event of its being impossible, it might involve the necessity of an embarrassing explanation. But the ghost sat down on the opposite side of the fireplace, as if he were quite used to it.

"You don't believe in me," observed the ghost.

"I don't," said Scrooge.

"What evidence would you have of my reality beyond that of your senses?"

"I don't know," said Scrooge.

"Why do you doubt your senses?"

"Because," said Scrooge, "a little thing affects them. A slight disorder of the stomach makes them cheats. You may be an undigested bit of beef, a blot of mustard, a crumb of cheese, a fragment of an underdone potato. There's more of gravy than of grave about you, whatever you are!"

Though the ghost sat perfectly motionless, its hair and skirts and tassels were still agitated as by the hot vapour from an oven.

"You see this toothpick?" said Scrooge, returning quickly to the charge, and wishing, though it were only for a second, to divert the vision's stony gaze from himself.

"I do," said the ghost.

"You are not looking at it," said Scrooge.

"But I see it," said the ghost, "notwithstanding."

"Well!" returned Scrooge. "I have but to swallow this and be for the rest of my days persecuted by a legion of goblins, all of my own creation. Humbug, I tell you — humbug!"

At this the spirit raised a frightful cry and shook its chain with such a dismal and appalling noise that Scrooge held on tight to his chair, to save himself from falling into a swoon. But how much greater was his horror when, the phantom taking off its bandage round its head as if it were too warm to wear indoors, its lower jaw dropped down upon its breast!

Scrooge fell upon his knees and clasped his hands before his face.

"Mercy!" he said. "Dreadful apparition, why do you trouble me?"

"Man of the worldly mind," replied the ghost, "do you believe in me or not?"

"I do," said Scrooge. "I must. But why do spirits walk the earth, and why do they come to me?"

"It is required of every man," the ghost returned, "that the spirit within him should walk abroad among his fellow-men, and travel far and wide; and if that spirit goes not forth in life, it is condemned to do so after death. It is doomed to wander through the world – oh, woe is me! – and witness what it cannot share, but might have shared on earth, and turned to happiness!"

Again the spectre raised a cry and shook its chain and wrung its shadowy hands.

"You are fettered," said Scrooge, trembling. "Tell me why!"

"I wear the chain I forged in my life," replied the ghost. "I made it link by link, yard by yard. I girded it on of my own free will and of my own free will I wore it. Is its pattern strange to you?"

Scrooge trembled more and more.

"Or would you know," pursued the ghost, "the weight and length of the strong coil you bear yourself? It was just as heavy and long as this seven Christmas Eves ago. You have laboured on it since. It is a ponderous chain!"

Scrooge glanced about him on the floor, in the expectation of finding himself surrounded by some fifty or sixty fathoms of iron cable; but he could see nothing.

"Jacob," he said imploringly. "Old Jacob Marley, tell me more. Speak comfort to me, Jacob!"

"I have none to give," the ghost replied. "It comes from other regions, Ebenezer Scrooge, and it is conveyed by other ministers to other kinds of men. Nor can I tell you what I would. A very little more is all that is permitted to me. I cannot rest, I cannot stay. My spirit never walked beyond our counting-house. Weary journeys lie before me!"

"You have been seven years dead," mused Scrooge, "and travelling all the time?"

"The whole time," said the ghost. "No rest, no peace. Incessant torture of remorse."

It held up its chain at arm's length as if that were the cause of all its unavailing grief, and flung it heavily upon the ground again.

"At this time of the year," the spectre said, "I suffer most.

Why did I walk through the crowds of fellow-beings with my eyes turned down, and never raise them to that blessed Star which led the Wise Men to a poor abode?"

Scrooge was much dismayed to hear the spectre going on at this rate, and began to quake exceedingly.

"Hear me!" cried the ghost. "My time is nearly gone."

"I will," said Scrooge. "But don't be hard on me, Jacob! Pray!"

"I am here tonight to warn you," continued the ghost, "that you yet have a chance of escaping my fate. A chance and a hope that lie in my power."

"You were always a good friend to me," said Scrooge. "Thank'ee."

"You will be haunted," resumed the ghost, "by three spirits."

Scrooge's countenance fell almost as low as the ghost's had done.

"Is that the chance and hope you mentioned, Jacob?" he demanded, in a faltering voice.

"It is."

"I – I think I'd rather not," said Scrooge.

"Without their visits," said the ghost, "you cannot hope to shun the path I tread. Expect the first tomorrow, when the bell tolls one."

"Couldn't I take 'em all at once and have it over, Jacob?" hinted Scrooge.

"Expect the second on the next night at the same hour. The third upon the next night when the last stroke of twelve has ceased to vibrate. Look to see me no more; and see that, for your sake, you remember what has passed between us!"

When Scrooge awoke it was so dark that, looking out of bed, he could scarcely distinguish the transparent window from the opaque walls of his room. He was endeavouring to pierce the darkness with his ferret eyes when the chimes of the neighbouring church struck the four quarters. So he listened for the hour.

To his great astonishment the heavy bell went on from six

to seven and from seven to eight and regularly up to twelve; then stopped. Twelve! It was past two when he went to bed. The clock was wrong. An icicle must have got into the works. Twelve!

He touched the spring of his repeater to correct this most preposterous clock. Its rapid little pulse beat twelve; and stopped.

"Why that isn't possible," said Scrooge, "that I can have slept through a whole day and far into another night. It isn't possible that anything has happened to the sun, and this is twelve at noon!"

Scrooge lay until the chime had gone three quarters more, when he remembered, on a sudden, that the ghost had warned him of a visitation when the bell tolled one. He resolved to lie awake until the hour was passed; and considering that he could no more go to sleep than go to heaven, this was perhaps the wisest resolution in his power.

The quarter was so long that he was more than once convinced that he must have sunk into a doze unconsciously and missed the clock. At length it broke upon his listening ear.

"Ding, dong!"

"A quarter past," said Scrooge, counting.

"Ding, dong!"

"Half-past!" said Scrooge.

"Ding, dong!"

"A quarter to it," said Scrooge.

"Ding, dong!"

"The hour itself," said Scrooge triumphantly, "and nothing else!"

He spoke before the hour bell sounded, which it now did with a deep, dull, hollow, melancholy ONE. Light flashed up in the room upon the instant, and the curtains of his bed were drawn.

The curtains of his bed were drawn aside, I tell you, by a hand. Not the curtains at his feet, nor the curtains at his back, but those to which his face was turned. The curtains of his bed were drawn aside; and Scrooge, starting up into a half-recumbent attitude, found himself face to face with the unearthly visitor, who drew them: as close to it as I am now to you, and I am standing in the spirit at your elbow.

It was a strange figure – like a child; yet not so like a child as like an old man, viewed through some supernatural medium which gave him the appearance of being diminished to a child's proportions. Its hair, which hung about its neck and down its back, was white as if with age and yet the face had not a wrinkle in it, and the tenderest bloom was on its skin. The arms were very long and muscular; the hands the same; as if its hold were of uncommon strength. Its legs and feet, most delicately formed, were, like those upper limbs, bare. It wore a tunic of the purest white; and round its waist was bound a lustrous belt, the sheen of which was beautiful. It held a branch of fresh green holly in its hand; and, in singular contradiction of that wintry emblem, had its dress trimmed with summer flowers. But the strangest thing about it was that from the crown of its head there sprang a bright clear jet of light, by which all this was visible; and which was doubtless the occasion of its using, in its duller moments, a great extinguisher for a cap, which it now held under its arm.

"Are you the spirit, sir, whose coming was foretold to me?" asked Scrooge.

"I am!"

The voice was soft and gentle.

"Who, and what are you?" Scrooge demanded.

"I am the Ghost of Christmas Past."

"Long past?" inquired Scrooge.

"No, your past."

Perhaps Scrooge could not have told anybody why, if anybody could have asked him, but he had a special desire to see the spirit in his cap; and begged him to be covered.

"What!" exclaimed the ghost, "would you so soon put out, with worldly hands, the light I give? Is it not enough that you are one of those whose worldly passions made this cap and forced me through whole trains of years to wear it low upon my brow?"

Scrooge reverently disclaimed all intention to offend and made bold to inquire what business brought the ghost there.

"Your welfare!" said the ghost.

Scrooge expressed himself much obliged but could not help thinking that a night of unbroken rest would have been more helpful to that end. The spirit must have heard him thinking, for it said immediately –

"Take heed!" It put out its strong hand as it spoke and clasped him gently by the arm. "Rise and walk with me!"

The grasp, though gentle as a woman's hand, was not to be resisted. He rose; but finding that the spirit made towards the window, clasped its robe in supplication.

"I am a mortal," Scrooge remonstrated, "and liable to fall."

"Bear but a touch of my hand *there*," said the spirit, laying it upon his heart, "and you shall be upheld in more than this!"

As the words were spoken, they passed through the wall and stood upon an open country road with fields on either side. The city had entirely vanished. The darkness and the mist had vanished with it, for it was a clear, cold, winter day, with snow upon the ground.

"Good Heaven!" said Scrooge, clasping his hands together, as he looked about him. "I was bred in this place. I was a boy here!"

The spirit gazed mildly upon him. Scrooge was conscious of a thousand odours floating in the air, each one connected with a thousand thoughts, and hopes, and joys, and cares long, long forgotten!

"Your lip is trembling," said the ghost. "And what is that upon your cheek?"

Scrooge muttered, with an unusual catching in his voice, that it was a pimple; and begged the ghost to lead him where he would.

"You recollect the way?" inquired the spirit.

"Remember it!" cried Scrooge with fervour; "I could walk it blindfold."

"Strange to have forgotten it for so many years!" observed the ghost. "Let us go on."

They walked along the road — Scrooge recognising every gate and post and tree — until a little market-town appeared in the distance, with its bridge, its church and winding river.

"The school is not quite deserted," said the ghost. "A solitary child, neglected by his friends, is left there still."

Scrooge said he knew it. And he sobbed.

They left the high-road by a well-remembered lane, and soon approached a mansion of dull red brick, with a little weathercock on the roof. It was a large house, but one of broken fortunes; for the spacious offices were little used, their walls were damp and mossy, their windows broken and their gates decayed. Fowls clucked and strutted in the stables; and the coach-houses and sheds were overrun with grass.

They went, the ghost and Scrooge, across the hall, to a door at the back of the house. It opened before them and disclosed a long, bare, melancholy room, made barer still by lines of plain deal forms and desks. At one of these a lonely boy was reading near a feeble fire; and Scrooge sat down upon a form, and wept to see his poor forgotten self as he had used to be.

The spirit touched him on the arm and pointed to his younger self, intent upon his reading. Suddenly a man, in foreign garments — wonderfully real and distinct to look at — stood outside the window, with an axe stuck in his belt, and leading by the bridle an ass laden with wood.

"Why, it's Ali Baba!" Scrooge exclaimed in ecstasy. "It's dear old honest Ali Baba! Yes yes, I know! One Christmas time, when yonder solitary child was left all alone, he *did* come, for the first time, just like that. Poor boy! And the Sultan's Groom turned upside-down by the Genii; there he is upon his head! Serve him right! I'm glad of it. What business had he to be married to the Princess?"

To hear Scrooge expending all the earnestness of his nature on such subjects, in a most extraordinary voice between laughing and crying, and to see his heightened and excited face, would have been a surprise to his business friends in the city, indeed.

The ghost smiled thoughtfully, and waved its hand, saying as it did so, "Let us see another Christmas!"

The ghost stopped at a certain warehouse door, and asked Scrooge if he knew it.

"Know it!" said Scrooge. "Wasn't I apprenticed here!"

They went in. At the sight of an old gentleman in a Welsh wig, sitting behind such a high desk that if he had been two inches taller he must have knocked his head against the ceiling, Scrooge cried in great excitement –

"Why, it's old Fezziwig! Bless his heart; it's Fezziwig alive again!"

Old Fezziwig laid down his pen, and looked up at the clock, which pointed to the hour of seven. He rubbed his hands; adjusted his capacious waistcoat; laughed all over himself, from his shoes to his organ of benevolence; and called out in a comfortable, oily, rich, fat, jovial voice –

"Yo, ho, there! Ebenezer! Dick!"

Scrooge's former self, now grown to a young man, came briskly in, accompanied by his fellow-'prentice.

"Dick Wilkins, to be sure!" said Scrooge to the ghost. "Bless me, yes. There he is. He was very much attached to me, was Dick. Poor Dick! Dear, dear!"

"Yo ho, my boys!" said Fezziwig. "No more work tonight. Christmas Eve, Dick. Christmas, Ebenezer! Let's have the shutters up," cried old Fezziwig, "before you can say Jack Robinson!" And skipping down from his high desk with wonderful agility, he continued, "Clear away, my lads, and let's have lots of room here!"

It was all done in a minute. Every movable was packed off, the floor was swept and watered, the lamps were trimmed, fuel was heaped upon the fire; and the warehouse was as snug, and warm, and dry, and bright a ballroom as you would desire to see upon a winter's night.

In came a fiddler with a music-book and went up to the lofty desk and made an orchestra of it, and tuned like fifty stomach-aches. In came Mrs. Fezziwig, one vast substantial smile. In came the three Misses Fezziwigs, beaming and lovable. In came the six young followers whose hearts they broke. In came all the young men and women employed in the business. In came the housemaid and her cousin, the baker. In came the cook, with her brother's particular friend, the milkman. In they all came, one after another, anyhow and everyhow. Away they all went, twenty couples at once; hands half round and back again the other way; down the middle and up again; round and round in various stages of affectionate grouping; old top couple always turning up in the wrong place; new top couple starting off again as soon as they got there. And at last old Fezziwig clapped his hands to stop the dancing and cried out, "Well done!" and the fiddler plunged his hot face into a pot of porter, especially provided for that purpose.

There were more dances and there were forfeits and more dances and there was cake and there was a great piece of cold roast and there was a great piece of cod boiled and there were mince pies and plenty of beer. But the great effect of the evening came after the roast and boiled, when the fiddler struck up "Sir Roger de Coverley". Then old Fezziwig stood out to dance with Mrs Fezziwig.

When the clock struck eleven, this domestic ball broke up. Mr and Mrs Fezziwig took their stations, one on either side of the floor, and shaking hands with every person individually, wished him or her A Merry Christmas. When everybody had retired but the two 'prentices, they did the same to them; and thus the cheerful voices died away, and the lads were left to their beds; which were under a counter in the back shop.

During the whole of this time, Scrooge had acted like a man out of his wits. His heart and soul were in the scene, and with his former self. He corroborated everything, remembered everything, enjoyed everything. It was not until now, when the bright faces of his former self and Dick were turned from them, that he remembered the ghost, and became conscious that it was looking full upon him, while the light upon its head burned very clear.

"A small matter," said the ghost, "to make these silly folk so full of gratitude."

"Small!" echoed Scrooge.

The spirit signed to him to listen to the two apprentices, who were pouring out their hearts in praise of Fezziwig; and when he had done so, said –

"Why! Is it not? He has spent a few pounds of your mortal money; three or four perhaps. Is that so much that he deserves this praise?"

"It isn't that," said Scrooge, heated by the remark, and speaking unconsciously like his former, not his latter, self. "It isn't that, spirit. He has the power to render us happy or unhappy. Say that his power lies in words or looks; in things so slight and insignificant that it is impossible to add and count 'em up – what then? The happiness he gives is quite as great as if it cost a fortune."

He felt the spirit's glance and stopped.

"What is the matter?" asked the ghost.

"Nothing particular," said Scrooge.

"Something, I think?" the ghost insisted.

"No," said Scrooge. "No. I should like to be able to say a word or two to my clerk just now. That's all."

He was conscious of being exhausted, and overcome by an irresistible drowsiness; and further of being in his own bed-room. He had barely time to reel to bed, before he sank into a heavy sleep.

Awaking in the middle of a prodigiously tough snore, and sitting up in bed to get his thoughts together, Scrooge had no occasion to be told that the bell was again upon the stroke of one.

Now being prepared for almost anything, he was not by any means prepared for nothing; and, consequently, when the bell struck one and no shape appeared, he was taken with a violent fit of trembling. Five minutes, ten minutes, a quarter of an hour went by, yet nothing came. All this time he lay upon his bed, the very core and centre of a blaze of ruddy light, which streamed upon it when the clock proclaimed the hour; and which, being only light, was more alarming than a dozen ghosts, as he was powerless to make out what it meant;

and was sometimes apprehensive that he might be at that very moment an interesting case of spontaneous combustion, without having the consolation of knowing it.

At last, however, he began to think that the source and secret of this ghostly light might be in the adjoining room, from whence, on further tracing it, it seemed to shine. He got up softly and shuffled in his slippers to the door.

The moment Scrooge's hand was on the lock, a strange voice called him by his name and bade him enter. He obeyed.

It was his own room. There was no doubt about that. But it had undergone a surprising transformation. The walls and ceiling were so hung with living green that it looked a perfect grove; from every part of which bright gleaming berries glistened. The crisp leaves of holly, mistletoe and ivy reflected back the light, as if so many little mirrors had been scattered there; and such a mighty blaze went roaring up the chimney as that dull hearth had never known in Scrooge's time, or Marley's, or for many and many a winter season gone. Heaped up on the floor, to form a kind of throne, were turkeys, geese, game, poultry, great joints of meat, sucking-pigs, long wreaths of sausages, mince pies, plum-puddings, barrels of oysters, red-hot chestnuts, cherry-cheeked apples, juicy oranges, luscious pears, immense twelfth cakes and seething bowls of punch that made the chamber dim with their delicious steam. In easy state upon the couch there sat a jolly giant glorious to see; who bore a glowing torch, in shape not unlike Plenty's horn, and held it up, high up, to shed its light on Scrooge as he came peeping round the door.

"Come in!" exclaimed the ghost. "Come in! and know me better, man!"

Scrooge entered timidly, and hung his head before this spirit. He was not the dogged Scrooge he had been; and though the spirit's eyes were clear and kind, he did not like to meet them.

"I am the Ghost of Christmas Present," said the spirit. "Look upon me!"

Scrooge reverently did so. It was clothed in one simple,

deep-green robe, bordered with fine fur. The garment hung so loosely on the figure that its capacious breast was bare. Its feet, observable beneath the ample folds of the garment, were also bare; and on its head it wore no other covering than a holly wreath, set here and there with shining icicles. Its dark-brown curls were long and free; free as its genial face, its sparkling eye, its open hand, its cheery voice and its joyful air.

"You have never seen the like of me before!" exclaimed the spirit.

"Never," answered Scrooge.

"Have never walked forth with the younger members of my family; meaning (for I am very young) my elder brothers born in these later years?" pursued the phantom.

"I don't think I have," said Scrooge. "I am afraid I have not. Have you had many brothers, spirit?"

"More than eighteen hundred," said the ghost.

"A tremendous family to provide for!" muttered Scrooge.

The Ghost of Christmas Present rose.

"Spirit," said Scrooge submissively, "conduct me where you will. I went forth last night on compulsion, and I learned a lesson which is working now. To-night, if you have aught to teach me, let me profit by it."

"Touch my robe!"

Scrooge did as he was told, and held it fast.

Holly, mistletoe, red berries, ivy, turkeys, geese, game, poultry, meat, pigs, sausages, oysters, pies, puddings, fruit and punch all vanished instantly. So did the room, the fire, the ruddy glow, the hour of night, and they stood in the city streets on Christmas morning, where (for the weather was severe) the people made a rough, but brisk and not unpleasant, kind of music, in scraping the snow from the pavement in front of their dwellings, and from the tops of their houses, whence it was mad delight to the boys to see it come plumping down into the road below, and splitting into artificial little snow-storms.

There was an air of cheerfulness in the town, for the people who were shovelling away on the housetops were jovial and full of glee; calling out to one another from the parapets, and now and then exchanging a facetious snowball, laughing heartily if it went right, and no less heartily if it went wrong. The poulterers' shops were still half open, and the fruiterers' were radiant in their glory. The grocers'! oh, the grocers'! nearly closed, with perhaps two shutters down or one; but through those gaps such glimpses! The customers were all so hurried and so eager in the hopeful promise of the day, that they tumbled up against each other at the door, crashing their wicker baskets wildly, and left their purchases upon the counter and came running back to fetch them, and committed hundreds of mistakes in the best manner possible.

Perhaps it was the pleasure the good spirit had in showing off this power of his, or else it was his own kind, generous, hearty nature and his sympathy with all poor men, that led him straight to Scrooge's clerk; for there he went and took Scrooge with him. And on the threshold of the door the spirit smiled, and stopped to bless Bob Cratchit's dwelling with the sprinklings of his torch.

Then up rose Mrs Cratchit, Cratchit's wife, dressed out but poorly in a twice-turned gown, but brave in ribbons, which are cheap and make a goodly show for sixpence; and she laid the cloth, assisted by Belinda Cratchit, second of her daughters, also brave in ribbons; while Master Peter Cratchit plunged a fork into the saucepan of potatoes, and getting the corners of his monstrous shirt-collar (Bob's private property conferred upon his son and heir in honour of the day) into his mouth, rejoiced to find himself so gallantly attired, and yearned to show his linen in the fashionable parks.

And now two smaller Cratchits, boy and girl, came tearing in, screaming that outside the baker's they had smelled the goose, and known it for their own; and basking in luxurious thoughts of sage and onion these young Cratchits danced about the table, and exalted Master Peter Cratchit to the skies, while he, (not proud, although his collars nearly choked him) blew the fire, until the slow potatoes bubbling up, knocked loudly at the saucepan-lid to be let out and peeled. "What has ever got your precious father then?" said Mrs Cratchit. "And your brother, Tiny Tim! And Martha warn't as late last Christmas Day by half an hour."

"Here's Martha, mother!" said a girl, appearing as she spoke.

"Here's Martha, mother!" cried the two young Cratchits. "Hurrah! There's *such* a goose, Martha!"

"Why, bless your heart alive, my dear, how late you are!" said Mrs Cratchit, kissing her a dozen times, and taking off her shawl and bonnet for her with officious zeal.

"We'd a deal of work to finish up last night," replied the girl, "and had to clear away this morning, mother!"

"Well! Never mind so long as you are come," said Mrs Cratchit. "Sit ye down before the fire, my dear, and have a warm, Lord bless ye!"

"No, no! There's father coming," cried the two young Cratchits, who were everywhere at once. "Hide, Martha, hide!"

So Martha hid herself, and in came little Bob, the father, with at least three feet of comforter exclusive of the fringe, hanging down before him; and his threadbare clothes darned up and brushed, to look seasonable; and Tiny Tim upon his shoulder. Alas for Tiny Tim, he bore a little crutch, and had his limbs supported by an iron frame!

"Why, where's our Martha?" cried Bob Cratchit, looking round.

"Not coming," said Mrs Cratchit.

"Not coming!" said Bob, with a sudden declension in high spirits; for he had been Tim's blood-horse all the way from church, and had come home rampant. "Not coming upon Christmas Day!"

Martha didn't like to see him disappointed, if it were only in joke; so she came out prematurely from behind the closed door and ran into his arms, while the two young Cratchits hustled Tiny Tim, and bore him off into the wash-house, that he might hear the pudding singing in the copper.

"And how did little Tim behave?" asked Mrs Cratchit, when she had rallied Bob on his credulity, and Bob had hugged his daughter to his heart's content.

"As good as gold," said Bob, "and better. Somehow he gets thoughtful, sitting by himself so much, and thinks the strangest things you ever heard. He told me, coming home, that he hoped the people saw him in church, because he was a cripple, and it might be pleasant to them to remember upon Christmas Day who made lame beggars walk and blind men see."

Bob's voice was tremulous when he told them this, and trembled more when he said that Tiny Tim was growing strong and hearty.

His active little crutch was heard upon the floor, and back came Tiny Tim before another word was spoken, escorted by his brother and sister to his stool beside the fire. Master Peter and the two ubiquitous young Cratchits went to fetch the goose, with which they soon returned in high procession.

Such a bustle ensued that you might have thought a goose was the rarest of all birds. Mrs Cratchit made the gravy in a little saucepan hissing hot; Master Peter mashed the potatoes with incredible vigour; Miss Belinda sweetened up the apple-sauce; Martha dusted the hot plates; Bob took Tiny Tim beside him in a tiny corner at the table; the two young Cratchits set chairs for everybody, not forgetting themselves, and mounting guard upon their posts, crammed spoons into their mouths, lest they should shriek for goose before their turn came to be helped.

At last the dishes were set on, and grace was said. It was succeeded by a breathless pause, as Mrs Cratchit, looking slowly all along the carving-knife, prepared to plunge it in the breast; but when she did, and when the long expected gush of stuffing issued forth, one murmur of delight rose all around the board, and even Tiny Tim, excited by the two young Cratchits, beat on the table with the handle of his knife, and feebly cried Hurrah!

There never was such a goose. Its tenderness and flavour, size and cheapness, were the themes of universal admiration. Eked out by apple-sauce and mashed potatoes, it was a sufficient dinner for the whole family.

But now, the plates being changed by Miss Belinda, Mrs Cratchit left the room alone – too nervous to bear witnesses – to take the pudding up, and bring it in.

Suppose it should not be done enough! Suppose it should break in turning out! Suppose somebody should have got over the wall of the backyard, and stolen it, while they were merry with the goose – a supposition at which the two young Cratchits became livid! All sorts of horrors were supposed.

Hallo! A great deal of steam! The pudding was out of the copper. A smell like washing-day! That was the cloth. A smell like an eating-house and a pastrycook's next door to each other, with a laundress's next door to that! That was the pudding! In half a minute Mrs Cratchit entered – flushed, but smiling proudly – with the pudding, like a speckled cannon-ball, so hard and firm, blazing in half of half a quartern of ignited brandy, and with Christmas holly stuck into the top.

Oh, a wonderful pudding! Bob Cratchit said calmly that he regarded it as the greatest success achieved by Mrs Cratchit since their marriage. Everybody had something to say about it but nobody said or thought that it was at all a small pudding for a large family.

At last the dinner was all done, the cloth was cleared, the hearth swept, and the fire made up. Then all the Cratchit family drew round the hearth, in what Bob Cratchit called a circle, meaning half a one; and at Bob Cratchit's elbow stood the family display of glass. Two tumblers, and a custard-cup without a handle. With beaming looks, Bob served out the steaming beverage, while the chestnuts on the fire sputtered and cracked noisily. Then Bob proposed:

"A Merry Christmas to us all, my dears. God bless us!"

Which all the family re-echoed.

"God bless us every one!" said Tiny Tim, the last of all.

He sat very close to his father's side, upon his little stool. Bob held his withered little hand in his, as if he loved the child, and wished to keep him by his side, and dreaded that he might be taken from him.

"Spirit," said Scrooge, with an interest he had never felt before, "tell me if Tiny Tim will live."

"I see a vacant seat," replied the ghost, "in the poor chimney-corner, and a crutch without an owner, carefully preserved. If these remain unaltered by the future, the child will die."

"No, no," said Scrooge. "Oh, no, kind spirit! Say he will be spared."

"If these shadows remain unaltered by the future, none other of my race," returned the ghost, "will find him here. What then? If he be like to die, he had better do it, and decrease the surplus population."

Scrooge hung his head to hear his own words quoted by the spirit, and was overcome with penitence and grief.

"Man," said the ghost, "if man you be in heart, forbear that wicked cant until you have discovered what the surplus is, and where it is. Will you decide what men shall live, what men shall die? It may be that in the sight of Heaven, you are more worthless and less fit to live than millions like this poor man's child."

Scrooge bent before the ghost's rebuke, and trembling, cast his eyes upon the ground. But he raised them speedily on hearing his own name. "Mr Scrooge!" said Bob; "I'll give you Mr Scrooge, the founder of the feast!"

"The founder of the feast indeed!" cried Mrs Cratchit, reddening. "I wish I had him here. I'd give him a piece of my mind to feast upon, and I hope he'd have a good appetite for it."

"My dear," said Bob, "the children! Christmas Day."

"It should be Christmas Day, I am sure," said she, "on which one drinks the health of such an odious, stingy, hard, unfeeling man as Mr Scrooge. You know he is, Robert! Nobody knows it better than you do, poor fellow!"

"My dear," was Bob's mild answer, "Christmas Day."

"I'll drink his health for your sake and the day's," said Mrs Cratchit, "not for his. Long life to him! A Merry Christmas and A Happy New Year! He'll be very merry and very happy, I have no doubt!"

The children drank the toast after her. It was the first of their proceedings which had no heartiness in it. Tiny Tim drank it last of all, but he didn't care twopence for it. Scrooge was the ogre of the family. The mention of his name cast a dark shadow on the party, which was not dispelled for full five minutes.

They were not a handsome family; they were not well dressed; their shoes were far from being waterproof; their clothes were scanty. But they were happy, grateful, pleased with one another, and contented with the time; and when they faded, and looked happier yet in the bright sprinklings of the spirit's torch at parting, Scrooge had his eye upon them, and especially on Tiny Tim, until the last.

[The spirit then led Scrooge to see how Christmas was being spent deep in the coal mines, up in the lighthouses and away on the high seas. Every one was making merry as best he could.

At last they reached the home of Scrooge's nephew.]

It was a great surprise to Scrooge to find himself in a bright, dry, gleaming room, with the spirit standing smiling by his side, and looking at that same nephew with approving affability!

"Ha, ha!" laughed Scrooge's nephew. "Ha, ha, ha!"

If you should happen, by any unlikely chance, to know a man more blessed in a laugh than Scrooge's nephew, all I can say is, I should like to know him too. Introduce him to me, and I'll cultivate his acquaintance.

There is nothing in the world so irresistibly contagious as laughter and good humour. When Scrooge's nephew laughed in this way – holding his sides, rolling his head, and twisting his face into the most extravagant contortions – Scrooge's niece, by marriage, laughed as heartily as he. And their assembled friends, being not a bit behindhand, roared out lustily.

"Ha, ha! Ha, ha, ha!"

"He said that Christmas was a humbug, as I live!" cried Scrooge's nephew. "He believed it, too!"

"More shame for him, Fred!" said Scrooge's niece indignantly.

"He's a comical old fellow," went on Scrooge's nephew, "that's the truth; and not as pleasant as he might be. However, his offences carry their own punishment, and I have nothing to say against him."

"I'm sure he's very rich, Fred," hinted Scrooge's niece. "At least, you always tell *me* so."

"What of that, my dear?" said Scrooge's nephew. "His wealth is of no use to him. He won't do any good with it. He doesn't make himself comfortable with it. He hasn't the satisfaction of thinking – ha, ha, ha! – that he's ever going to benefit us with it."

"I have no patience with him," observed Scrooge's niece.

"Oh, I have!" said Scrooge's nephew. "I am sorry for him; I couldn't be angry with him if I tried. Who suffers by his ill whims? Himself, always. Here, he takes it into his head to dislike us, and he won't come and dine with us. What's the consequence? He don't lose much of a dinner."

"Indeed, I think he loses a very good dinner," interrupted Scrooge's niece and everybody else agreed.

"Well! I am very glad to hear it," said Scrooge's nephew, and he revelled in another great laugh.

"Do go on, Fred," said Scrooge's niece. "He never finishes what he begins to say! He is such a ridiculous fellow!"

"I was only going to say," said Scrooge's nephew, "that the consequence of his taking a dislike to us, and not making merry with us, is that he loses some pleasant moments which could do him no harm. I mean to give him the same chance every year, whether he likes it or not, for I pity him. He may rail at Christmas till he dies, but he can't help thinking better of it if he finds me going there, in good temper, year after year and saying, Uncle Scrooge, how are you? If it only puts him in the vein to leave his poor clerk fifty pounds, *that's* something; and I think I shook him yesterday."

After tea, they had some music and played a new game called Yes and No, where Scrooge's nephew had to think of something, and the rest must find out what; he only answering to their questions "yes" or "no," as the case was. The brisk fire of questioning to which he was exposed, elicited from him that he was thinking of an animal, a live animal, rather a disagreeable animal, a savage animal, an animal that growled and grunted sometimes, and talked sometimes, and lived in London, and walked about the streets, and wasn't made a show of, and wasn't led by anybody, and didn't live in a menagerie, and was never killed in a market, and was not a horse, or an ass, or a cow, or a bull, or a tiger, or a dog, or a pig, or a cat, or a bear. At every fresh question that was put to him, this nephew burst into a fresh roar of laughter; and was so inexpressibly tickled, that he was obliged to get up off the sofa and stamp. At last Scrooge's niece cried out:

"I have found it out! I know what it is, Fred! I know what it is!"

"What is it?" cried Fred.

"It's your uncle Scro-o-o-o-oge!"

Which it certainly was. Admiration was the universal sentiment, though some objected that the reply to "Is it a bear?" ought to have been "Yes".

"He has given us plenty of merriment, I am sure," said Fred, "and it would be ungrateful not to drink his health. Here is a glass of mulled wine ready to our hand at the moment; and I say, 'Uncle Scrooge!'"

"Well! Uncle Scrooge!" they cried.

"A Merry Christmas and A Happy New Year to the old man, whatever he is!" said Scrooge's nephew. "He wouldn't take it from me, but may he have it, nevertheless. Uncle Scrooge!"

Uncle Scrooge had imperceptibly become so gay and light of heart that he would have thanked them in an inaudible speech, if the ghost had given him time. But the whole scene passed off in the breath of the last word spoken by his nephew; and he and the spirit were again upon their travels.

Much they saw, and far they went. It was a long night, if it were only a night; but Scrooge had his doubts about this, because the Christmas holidays appeared to be condensed into the space of time they passed together. It was strange, too, that while Scrooge remained unaltered in his outward

form, the ghost grew older, clearly older. Scrooge had observed this change but never spoke of it, until they left a child's
Twelfth Night Party, when, looking at the spirit as they stood
together in an open space he noticed that its hair was grey.

"Are spirits' lives so short?" asked Scrooge.

"My life upon this globe is very brief," replied the ghost. "It
ends to-night."

"To-night!" cried Scrooge.

"To-night at midnight. Hark! The time is drawing near."

The bell struck twelve.

Scrooge looked about for the ghost, and saw it not. As the
last stroke ceased to vibrate, he remembered the prediction of
old Jacob Marley, and lifting up his eyes, beheld a solemn
phantom, draped and hooded, coming like a mist along the
ground, towards him.

The phantom slowly, gravely, silently approached. When it
came near him, Scrooge bent down upon his knee; for in the
very air through which this spirit moved it seemed to scatter
gloom and mystery.

It was shrouded in a deep-black garment, which concealed
its head, its face, its form, and left nothing of it visible save one
outstretched hand. But for this it would have been difficult to
detach its figure from the night, and separate it from the
darkness by which it was surrounded.

He felt that it was tall and stately when it came beside him,
and that its mysterious presence filled him with a solemn
dread. He knew no more, for the spirit neither spoke nor
moved.

"I am in the presence of the Ghost of Christmas Yet to
Come?" said Scrooge.

The spirit answered not, but pointed onward with its hand.

"Lead on!" said Scrooge. "Lead on! The night is waning fast,
and it is precious time to me, I know. Lead on, spirit!"

The phantom moved away as it had come towards him.
Scrooge followed in the shadow of its dress, which bore him
up, he thought, and carried him along.

[The phantom showed the future, and Scrooge heard what people were saying of a much disliked man who had recently died. He even saw how the man's home, his furnishings and belongings were stolen even while his body lay cold in the house. No one cared a rap about this friendless, unfortunate man.]

"Spectre," said Scrooge, "something informs me that our parting moment is at hand. I know it but I know not how. Tell me what man that was whom we saw lying dead?"

The Ghost of Christmas Yet to Come conveyed him, as before – though at a different time, he thought: indeed there seemed no order in these latter visions, save that they were in the future – into the resorts of business men, but showed him not himself.

Scrooge hastened to the window of his office, and looked in. It was an office still, but not his. The furniture was not the same, and the figure in the chair was not himself. The phantom pointed as before.

He joined it once again, and wondering why and whither he had gone, accompanied it until they reached an iron gate. He paused to look round before entering.

A churchyard. Here, then, the wretched man whose name he had now to learn lay underneath the ground. It was a worthy place. Walled in by houses; overrun by grass and weeds, the growth of vegetation's death, not life; choked up with too much burying; fat with rejected appetite. A worthy place!

The spirit stood among the graves, and pointed down to one. He advanced towards it, trembling. The phantom was exactly as it had been, but he dreaded that he saw new meaning in its solemn shape.

"Before I draw nearer to that stone to which you point," said Scrooge, "answer me one question. Are these the shadows of the things that will be, or are they the shadows of the things that may be, only?"

Still the ghost pointed downward to the grave by which it stood.

Scrooge crept towards it, trembling as he went; and follow-

ing the finger, read upon the stone of the neglected grave his own name, EBENEZER SCROOGE.

"Am *I* the man who lay upon the bed?" he cried, upon his knees.

The finger pointed from the grave to him, and back again.

"No, spirit! Oh, no, no!"

The finger was still there.

"Spirit!" he cried, tight clutching at its robe, "hear me. I am not the man I was. I will not be the man I must have been but for this meeting. Why show me this, if I am past all hope?"

For the first time the hand appeared to shake.

"Good spirit," he pursued, as down upon the ground he fell before it, "your nature intercedes for me, and pities me. Assure me that I yet may change these shadows you have shown me, by an altered life!"

The kind hand trembled.

"I will honour Christmas in my heart, and try to keep it all the year. I will live in the past, the present, and the future. The spirits of all three shall strive within me. I will not shut out the lessons that they teach. Oh, tell me I may sponge away the writing on this stone!"

In his agony, he caught the spectral hand. It sought to free itself, but he was strong in his entreaty, and detained it. The spirit, stronger yet, repulsed him.

Holding up his hand in a last prayer to have his fate reversed, he saw an alteration in the phantom's hood and dress. It shrank, collapsed, and dwindled down into a bedpost.

Yes! and the bedpost was his own. The bed was his own. Best and happiest of all, the time before him was his own, to make amends in!

"I will live in the past, the present, and the future!" Scrooge repeated, as he scrambled out of bed. "The spirits of all three shall strive within me. O Jacob Marley! Heaven and Christmas time be praised for this! I say it on my knees, old Jacob; on my knees!"

He was so fluttered and so glowing with his good intentions, that his broken voice would scarcely answer to his call. He had been sobbing violently in his conflict with the spirit, and his face was wet with tears.

His hands were busy with his clothes; turning them inside out, putting them on upside down, tearing them and mislaying them.

"I don't know what to do!" cried Scrooge, laughing and crying in the same breath. "I am as light as a feather, as happy as an angel, as merry as a schoolboy. A Merry Christmas to everybody! A Happy New Year to all the world. Hallo, here! Whoop! Hallo!"

He had frisked into the sitting-room and was now standing there, perfectly winded.

"There's the saucepan that the gruel was in!" cried Scrooge, starting off again, and going round the fireplace. "There's the door, by which the Ghost of Jacob Marley entered! There's the corner where the Ghost of Christmas Present sat! It's all right, it's all true, it all happened. Ha, ha, ha!"

Really, for a man who had been out of practice for so many years, it was a splendid laugh, a most illustrious laugh. The father of a long, long line of brilliant laughs!

"I don't know what day of the month it is!" said Scrooge. "I don't know how long I've been among the spirits. I don't know anything. I'm quite a baby. Never mind. I don't care. I'd rather be a baby. Hallo! Whoop! Hallo, here!"

Running to the window, he opened it and put out his head. No fog, no mist; clear, bright, jovial, stirring, cold; cold, piping for blood to dance to; golden sunlight; heavenly sky; sweet fresh air; merry bells. Oh, glorious. Glorious!

"What's to-day?" cried Scrooge, calling downward to a boy in Sunday clothes, who perhaps had loitered in to look about him.

"Eh?" returned the boy, with all his might of wonder.

"What's to-day, my fine fellow?" said Scrooge.

"To-day!" replied the boy. "Why, CHRISTMAS DAY."

"It's Christmas Day!" said Scrooge to himself. "I haven't missed it. The spirits have done it all in one night. They can do

anything they like. Of course they can. Of course they can.
Hallo, my fine fellow!"

"Hallo!" returned the boy.

"Do you know the poulterer's in the next street but one, at
the corner?"

"I should hope I did," replied the lad.

"An intelligent boy!" said Scrooge. "A remarkable boy! Do
you know whether they've sold the prize turkey that was
hanging up there? Not the little prize turkey; the big one?"

"What, the one as big as me?" returned the boy.

"What a delightful boy!" said Scrooge. "It's a pleasure to
talk to him. Yes, my buck!"

"It's hanging there now," replied the boy.

"Is it?" said Scrooge. "Go and buy it."

"Wh-a-a-t!" exclaimed the boy.

"I am in earnest," said Scrooge. "Go and buy it, and tell 'em
to bring it here, that I may give them the direction where to
take it. Come back with the man and I'll give you a shilling.
Come back in less than five minutes, and I'll give you half a
crown!"

The boy was off like a shot. "I'll send it to Bob Cratchit's!"
whispered Scrooge, splitting with a laugh. "He shan't know
who sends it. It's twice the size of Tiny Tim."

The hand in which he wrote the address was not a steady
one, but write it he did, somehow, and went downstairs to
open the street door, ready for the coming of the poulterer's
man. As he stood there, waiting his arrival, the knocker
caught his eye.

"I shall love it as long as I live!" cried Scrooge, patting it
with his hand. "I scarcely ever looked at it before. What an
honest expression it has in its face. It's a wonderful knocker.
Here's the turkey. Hallo! How are you? Merry Christmas!"

It *was* a turkey! He could never have stood upon his legs,
that bird. He would have snapped 'em short off in a minute,
like sticks of sealing-wax.

"Why, it's impossible to carry that to Camden Town," said
Scrooge. "You must have a cab."

The chuckle with which he said this, and the chuckle with which he paid for the turkey, and the chuckle with which he paid for the cab, and the chuckle with which he recompensed the boy, were only to be exceeded by the chuckle with which he sat down breathless, and chuckled till he cried.

He dressed himself "all in his best", and at last got out into the streets. The people were by this time pouring forth, as he had seen them with the Ghost of Christmas Present; Scrooge regarded every one with a delighted smile. He looked so irresistibly pleasant, in a word, that three or four good-humoured fellows said "Good-morning, sir. A Merry Christmas to you!" And Scrooge said often afterwards that he had never heard sounds more blithe.

He had not gone far, when coming on towards him he beheld the portly gentleman who had walked into his counting-house the day before, and said, "Scrooge and Marley's, I believe?" It sent a pang across his heart to think how this old gentleman would look upon him when they met; but he knew what path lay straight before him, and he took it.

"My dear sir," said Scrooge, quickening his pace and taking the old gentleman by both his hands. "How do you do? I hope you succeeded yesterday. It was very kind of you. A Merry Christmas to you, sir!"

"Mr Scrooge?"

"Yes," said Scrooge, "That is my name, and I fear it may not be pleasant to you. Allow me to ask your pardon. And will you have the goodness – " here Scrooge whispered in his ear.

"Lord bless me!" cried the gentleman, as if his breath were taken away. "My dear Mr Scrooge, are you serious?"

"If you please," said Scrooge. "Not a farthing less. A great many back payments are included in it."

"My dear sir," said the other, shaking hands with him. "I don't know what to say to such munifi – "

"Don't say anything, please," retorted Scrooge. "Come and see me. Will you come and see me?"

"I will!" cried the old gentleman. And it was clear he meant to do it.

"Thank'ee," said Scrooge. "I am much obliged to you. I thank you fifty times. Bless you!"

He went to church, and walked about the streets, patted children on the head, questioned beggars, and found that everything could yield him pleasure. In the afternoon he turned his steps towards his nephew's house.

He passed the door a dozen times, before he had the courage to go up and knock. But he made a dash and did it.

"Is your master at home, my dear?" said Scrooge to the girl. Nice girl! Very.

"Yes, sir."

"Where is he, my love?" said Scrooge.

"He's in the dining-room, along with mistress. I'll show you upstairs."

"Thank'ee. He knows me," said Scrooge, with his hand already on the dining-room lock. "I'll go in there, my dear."

He turned it gently, and sidled his face in, round the door. "Fred!" said Scrooge.

Dear heart alive, how his niece by marriage started!

"Why, bless my soul!" cried Fred. "Who's that?"

"It's I. Your uncle Scrooge. I have come to dinner. Will you let me in, Fred?"

Let him in! It is a mercy he didn't shake his arm off. He was at home in five minutes. Nothing could be heartier. Everyone was hearty. Wonderful party, wonderful games, wonderful happiness.

But he was early at the office next morning. Oh, he was early there. If he could only be there first, and catch Bob Cratchit coming late! That was the thing he had set his heart upon.

And he did it; yes he did! The clock struck nine. No Bob. A quarter past. No Bob. He was full eighteen minutes and a half behind his time. Scrooge sat with his door open, that he might see him come into the tank.

His hat was off before he opened the door. He was on his stool in a jiffy; driving away with his pen, as if he were trying to overtake nine o'clock.

"Hallo!" growled Scrooge in his accustomed voice, as near as he could feign it. "What do you mean by coming here at this time of day?"

"I am very sorry, sir," said Bob. "I *am* behind my time."

"You are?" repeated Scrooge. "Yes. I think you are. Step this way."

"It's only once a year, sir," pleaded Bob, appearing from the tank. "It shall not be repeated. I was making rather merry yesterday, sir."

"Now, I'll tell you what, my friend," said Scrooge; "I am not going to stand this sort of thing any longer. And therefore," he continued, leaping from his stool, and giving Bob such a dig in the waistcoat that he staggered back into the tank again; "and therefore I am about to raise your salary!"

Bob trembled, and got a little nearer to the ruler. He had a momentary idea of knocking Scrooge down with it, holding him, and calling to the people in the court for help and a strait waistcoat.

"A Merry Christmas, Bob!" said Scrooge, with an earnestness that could not be mistaken, as he clapped him on the back. "A merrier Christmas, Bob, my good fellow, than I have given you for many a year. I'll raise your salary, and endeavour to assist your struggling family, and we will discuss your affairs this very afternoon, over a Christmas bowl of smoking bishop, Bob! Make up the fires, and buy another coal-scuttle before you dot another i, Bob Cratchit!"

Scrooge was better than his word. He did it all and infinitely more; and to Tiny Tim, who did NOT die, he was a second father. He became as good a friend, as good a master, and as good a man, as the good old city knew. Some people laughed to see the alteration in him, but he let them laugh and little heeded them. His own heart laughed; and that was quite enough for him.

He had no further encounters with spirits; and it was always said of him that he knew how to keep Christmas as well as any man. May that be truly said of all of us! And so, as Tiny Tim observed, God bless us every one!

[Dickens, of course, is not to be trifled with. How could one dare to let the reader down by presenting an altered or mutilated version of this immortal story? To find room for it in this collection some cuts were necessary, but don't, please, think of it as a shortened version, but rather as one in which the full robust flavour of the original has been retained despite one or two changes in the wording and minuscule omissions of those entrancingly interminable embellishments which are part of the master's uniqueness. Stephen Corrin]

THE GHOST OF CHRISTMAS PRESENT

WENDY EYTON

[If you have read A Christmas Carol *you will recognize the ghost in this story.]*

"I spy with my little eye, something beginning with 'S'," said Gus.

"Slalom Super Surfer," said Charlie.

"There's no Slalom Super Surfer around here. You've got skateboards on the brain, Charlie."

"S for SPLAT, then," said Charlie, giving a large, over-ripe tomato a hefty kick. It shot straight out of the gutter, where it had rolled from an over-loaded fruit and vegetable barrow.

"You'll pay for that," yelled the man at the barrow, turning as purple as his "Special Offer Christmas Grapes".

A mighty crash, a shower of brickdust and splinters, sent the two boys racing to the corner of the street.

"It's coming down,' cried Gus. "The old house is coming down. The big bull's after it."

For weeks workmen had been tapping at the building, the last but one of a row of Victorian terraced houses, and now the yellow bull-dozer was finishing off the job. From clouds of grey dust the inner wall of the house merged in patches of different colours, wallpaper torn and flapping. Gus gazed up in awe at what had been the wall of a bedroom for perhaps a hundred years. There was still an old shelf moulded to the wall and, miraculously, a glass bottle with a slender neck was standing on the shelf. As the bull-dozer heaved and clanked towards its victim, eager for the final kill, the bottle fell to the ground and smashed. Gus thought he saw a big, white bird rise from the ruins of the house into the clear December sky.

"Hey, Charlie, did you see that?" he called excitedly, but Charlie, deep in imaginary one-wheeler kick turns, was already out of hearing distance. Gus caught up with him at the amusement park.

One half of the amusement park had been converted into an East London Skateopia. Now it lay deserted, its surface eerily pitted, like some lunar landscape.

"Who'd want to use it in this weather?" said Gus, shivering. "Or when it's raining? I'd rather roller-skate at the disco."

"You can buy wheels now for special control in wet or dry weather," Charlie answered. "Why are you always moaning about the cold? Are you missing that Trinidad sun, man?"

"Guess so, man," said Gus, who had been born in Bermondsey.

When they reached home the winter sun was already throwing shadows across the courtyard of the flats and Mrs Ogilvie was standing in the main entrance, arms akimbo, thin legs firmly planted in enormous furry slippers.

Both boys had tangled in the past with Mrs Ogilvie. She had caught Charlie writing "Road Riders are Radical" inside one of the telephone kiosks, and taken Gus to task for what she called "Molestin' Trees".

The tree was a shivering morsel of vegetation between the high, windy blocks of flats. Someone had pushed a Coca-Cola can down inside the wire-netting surrounding the tree so that the rim of the can pushed into its bark. Gus had been trying to pull the can out when Mrs Ogilvie had spotted him. She spotted him now, her eyes alight with battle fervour.

"I'll have you for this,' she screeched. "Molestin' my windows. I'll get you this time."

"What's she on about?" muttered Charlie.

There was a message drawn across Mrs Ogilvie's front window in huge sprawling letters. The boys did not like to move close enough to read the writing.

· "Christmas is Humbug, is it?" screamed Mrs Ogilvie. "I'll give you Humbug."

Gus's mother came out of her flat into the entrance hall.

"Your lad's been at it again," shouted Mrs Ogilvie. "This time it's the window. Spent all day decorating for my daughter coming and the kids. Four pounds fifty that tinsel tree cost and then your lad starts plastering things across the window so folks can't see in."

"Mum, I haven't touched her window," said Gus. "And anyway I don't know what it means."

"Nor me," said Charlie. "I haven't touched her window, I haven't been near her blooming tinsel tree, and I don't know what 'Christmas is Humbug' means either."

"There you are then," said Gus's mother. "If my son says he hasn't touched your window I believe him. Charlie, too. And apart from anything else, that window of yours is at least five feet off the ground. Are you suggesting they used a ladder? Or stilts perhaps?"

"Humbugs," sneered Mrs Ogilvie, "as well as being mint lumps, is folks pretending to be what they're not."

She slammed her door.

"So long, Gus," said Charlie. "I'm going to see if ANYTHING's arrived. They were out shopping today." He went up the emergency stairs two at a time.

"Charlie's mum and dad are buying him a skateboard for Christmas," said Gus, "now the shops are selling them cheap."

"Lucky old Charlie," said his mother. "Let's hope he's having a helmet and knee-pads, too."

"I'd rather have a pair of roller-skates," Gus hinted.

"No, Gus, I've told you. All this traffic. It's not safe around here for roller-skates or skateboards either.' Gus's mother pushed him into their flat and closed the door. 'Oh, come on! Don't look so glum. With presents, it's the thought that counts. What did I say, now?"

"Mum," whispered Gus, staring beyond his mother's arrangement of red candles, ribbon and holly, "there's writing on our window, too."

The message was written on the outside of the window, and so appeared the wrong way round. Gus ran to get the bathroom mirror. It was written in the same style as the message on Mrs. Ogilvie's window. It was sprawling, and rather old-fashioned in style.

"What . . . reason . . . have you . . . to be . . . merry?" he read slowly, through the mirror. "You're . . . poor enough."

"Well, what a cheek!" said his mother. "Do you think it's that nasty woman getting her own back?"

Gus had a mental picture of Mrs Ogilvie's spindly legs on circus stilts.

Charlie was taking the concrete stairs three at a time now. He hoped his mum and dad had remembered about the oak deck with kicktail, and multi-coloured wheels. Later he would get a shiny orange helmet, and a jacket with multi-coloured stripes.

"Look out, Bobby Piercey," yelled Charlie, leaping to the top of the fourth flight and hurling himself round the corner. He came to an abrupt stop and gazed in bewilderment at the slightly frosted window at the top of the next flight of stairs. It looked as if someone had been painting on that window as well. But not words this time. Someone had painted a face on the window. Charlie climbed slowly, squinting at the face. It seemed to be that of an old man with white eyebrows. Was it supposed to be Father Christmas, Charlie wondered? He saw, on getting nearer, that the man had something peculiar on his head. Definitely not a hood, but more like a night-cap. That was it. Charlie remembered pictures he had seen in books about the old days. Men had worn caps to go to bed in at night, woollen caps with tassels or pom-poms. The face was very disagreeable, with its thin blue lips and pinched, pointed nose. Without quite knowing why, except perhaps from sheer dislike, Charlie put out his tongue at the face. It seemed to glare more ferociously than ever. And then something happened which shocked Charlie so much he nearly fell down the stairs. The face put its tongue out at Charlie – and disappeared. For a moment Charlie was unable to move in disbelief, then he ran up to the window. There was not a mark on it. He gazed through the window. There was no one to be seen. He was four and a half floors up and could make out no possible ledge on which anyone could have been standing.

"A trick of the light," thought Charlie. "What else could it have been?"

He continued up the stairs slowly, thinking. Charlie's flat was on floor six, but by the fifth floor he could already hear his young brother and sister crying, his mum shouting at them, and his dad shouting at his mum.

Charlie took advantage of the pandemonium to go into the big bedroom. The parcel on the bed held a doll's dressing outfit for Dawn. In the plastic bag on the chair he found cowboy boots for Wayne, a jigsaw puzzle, a packet of liquorice allsorts and a box of jelly bears. So intent on his quest was Charlie that he did not even think to take a jelly bear. He was about to begin a systematic skateboard search, starting under the bed and progressing through each dressing-table drawer, when noises on the landing disturbed him. He recognized the voice of Old Mrs Merritt, who lived in the flat directly below theirs. Old Mrs Merritt, excitable at the best of times, now seemed on the edge of hysteria.

"All right, I'll just get my cardigan and come down and have a look," Charlie heard his mother say. She flung open her bedroom door and eyed her son.

"Out," she said, pointing firmly, but not before Charlie had noticed her automatic glance to the top of the wardrobe at the hat she had bought for Auntie Brenda's wedding.

"So that's where she's put it," thought Charlie. "Under the hat."

Mrs Merritt, it seemed, had confronted the face of a man at her window, five floors up, and before long the whole block of flats was humming with news of similar sightings and anti-festive messages scrawled on windows, doors and even, in one instance, across the bonnet of a car.

It was generally agreed that the window-cleaner, in the absence of his suspension swing, could hardly be to blame.

Sixty per cent of the tenants came out in favour of a ghostly apparition and forty per cent in favour of a visitation from outer space. It was decided by one and all that a meeting should be called to discuss the matter, and the tenants of Jubilee block agreed to meet in the basement area at seven that evening.

"I suppose we ought to go, Alan," said Charlie's mother to Charlie's father at tea-time, rescuing a jam spoon which Wayne was just about to put in his mouth. "After all, it might be burglars. Charlie can stay here and look after Dawn and Wayne."

There was a tap on the door and Gus came in, full of repressed excitement and importance.

"I'm going to speak at the meeting," he told them, "because I think I know where that ghost came from. It came from out of a bottle!"

"Out of a bottle?" said Charlie's mother, wiping Wayne's sticky fingers in disbelief.

"Don't you remember, Charlie? That old house they were knocking down today? There was still a shelf left on the wall, and on the shelf I saw a glass bottle. When it smashed to the ground I thought I saw a big white bird fly up. But it could have been a ghost, Charlie. My mum says they keep spirits in bottles, sometimes."

"Only one kind of a spirit I know of in a bottle," said Charlie's dad. "Give him a cup of tea, Margaret. Quieten him down."

But Gus was too excited to drink tea.

"Everyone who's seen this ghost says he's wearing a nightcap and white nightshirt. That could look just like a big white bird, couldn't it? He must be real cold out there in his nightshirt after being in a bottle for more than a hundred years."

Charlie had been wondering whether or not to mention the face he had seen at the staircase window, but now he decided definitely against it. He didn't want to be forced to attend the tenant's meeting. With everyone herded together in the basement, with the top half of the block empty apart from Dawn, Wayne and himself, he had something far more important to do.

"What's got into you?" said his mother suspiciously when he offered to help her wash the tea-things.

At ten to seven he heard the other people from the top-floor flats chattering excitedly as they boarded the lift to the basement, but still his mum and dad hadn't gone.

"Sure you won't be scared up here alone, Charlie, with a ghost about?"

Charlie looked at his father in surprise. He hadn't even thought about it.

"Your mind on something else?" said his father. He winked at Charlie, put on an invisible Easter bonnet, and gave him the thumbs up sign.

When Charlie was quite sure his mother and father were at the meeting, and were not going to come back for anything, he went into their bedroom, stood on the chair, and took down a paper parcel from underneath his mother's hat. He was rather surprised to find the parcel still there, but he supposed that in the excitement over the ghost his mother had forgotten to move it to a second hiding-place. With trembling fingers he untied the knotted string and withdrew the smooth, gleaming skateboard. At first Charlie felt disappointment that the wheels were blue, but he quickly decided that a blue helmet, and a jacket with blue and orange stripes on the sleeve would be just the thing. He peeped into the adjoining bedroom, where Dawn was asleep and Wayne was busy tearing apart his Action Man. He closed the bedroom door firmly, put on a thick sweater, and crept up the stairs and on to the outer landing of the top floor of the flats.

The air was freezing and over the four-foot-high concrete barrier he could see, for miles and miles, the twinkling lights of London. Here and there loomed massive, darkened office blocks, and he could just make out, standing on his toes, the line of St. Paul's Cathedral in the distance.

"Mum would skin me alive," he thought, shivering with cold.

Charlie was not as adept on the skateboard as he liked Gus to think. Elaborate tail and nose wheelies were all right in the imagination. In practice he found it difficult to keep a firm foot, even in the middle of the skateboard.

As he skidded and tipped and slid past the empty flats, Charlie gradually became aware that he was not, after all, the only person up there that night. A silent figure, in ghostly grey nightshirt, nightcap and slippers, was watching him with an extremely disagreeable expression on its face. Strangely, after the first stab of shock, Charlie's feelings were less of fear than annoyance. He had no more than half an hour of precious freedom to try out his skateboard and this miserable old man had to come and spoil it all.

Why can't he go and haunt downstairs, where they're all talking about him? thought Charlie.

The ghost was semi-transparent. Charlie could see the lights of London dimly through that part of him which rose above the barrier. It was the biting wind, rather than terror, which stirred the hair on Charlie's head, but the ghost seemed unruffled by it. Charlie remembered Gus's remark about how cold the ghost must be after a hundred years or more in a tight, glass bottle.

"Not a very warm night," he said.

The ghost continued to glare at him. Charlie recognized the face as the one he had seen through the window. It was not quite as old as he had at first thought. Its eyebrows were not so much white as covered in snow.

"Oh, well, be like that," said Charlie. "Christmas isn't half as bad as you seem to think. This skateboard is a Christmas present, for instance. Now watch this, ghost."

He took a running leap on to the skateboard, which slipped from under him. As Charlie keeled over backwards the ghost emitted a hollow spectral snigger.

"You could do better, I suppose?" said Charlie, puffing and red in the face.

The ghost looked hesitantly at the skateboard, hovered over it in a tremulous fashion, and settled itself with one shimmering slippered foot on the deck.

"Go on then, Granddad, have a go," said Charlie.

The ghost looked at him uncertainly, and then its face broke into an unexpected, rather pleasant smile.

"Hollo, hoop, hollo! Yoho!" cried the ghost and shot past Charlie, in a flurry of tassel and nightshirt, up over the concrete barrier and into the darkness below.

"Come back here, that's my skateboard," yelled Charlie, but the ghost was receding farther and farther into the distance, from roof to rampart, from pillar to parking-meter, with faint and cheerful cries of "Chirrup" and "Hilli-ho".

Charlie's first thought was to chase after him, but there were sounds of other activity coming from below. He hurried back down the steps and into his bedroom, improvised a paper parcel around a pair of old sneakers, ran into his mother's room and pushed it under the hat. He darted into the livingroom and switched on the television set just as his mother came in.

"Waste of time, if you ask me," she said, flinging off her cardigan and flopping on to the settee. "They won't get any exorcist to come until after Christmas, that's for sure. And heaven knows what might happen in the meantime."

"What's an exorcist?" asked Charlie, his heart still thumping noisily.

"Someone who gets rid of evil spirits. Might even be able to put the old ghost back into a glass bottle, like the one Gus was talking about," said his father.

Charlie was not at all sure that the ghost was an evil spirit.

"But if they make him go back into a bottle, he won't be able to take my skateboard with him," he thought.

Charlie's dreams that night were haunted by skateboarding phantoms. He awoke in the morning to find frost as thick as icing across his bedroom window, and a message etched in the frost. The message was difficult to read backwards, as the letters were already melting into each other, but he finally made it out as:

"MERRY CHRISTMAS, CHARLIE. HOPE YOU WON'T BE
BORED WITHOUT YOUR
BOARD. HA-HA. EBENEZER S."

Charlie heard his mother coming into the room and drew the curtain quickly. His mother was full of the news that someone had written:

"THEN HEIGH-HO THE HOLLY
THIS LIFE IS MOST JOLLY!"

in letters two feet high across their living-room window, and throughout the Jubilee block that morning people found, in place of the former disgruntled messages, "PEACE AND GOODWILL", "SEASON'S GREETINGS TO YE" and once, rather unaccountably, "I HAVE GONE TO SKATE ON CORNHILL".

Mrs Ogilvie's tinsel tree mysteriously acquired gold baubles and Gus's mother's candles were found to be burning brightly, as if lit by some unseen hand.

Charlie was anxious to discover if the face had reappeared but no one, it seemed, had come across the ghost in person that day. Old Mrs Merritt screamed once at the sight of a large, moving blob of white outside her window, but it turned out to be no more than a melting snowball.

Snow had fallen heavily throughout the night.

"It looks like a great block of ice-cream," said Gus, running from the flats and looking upwards. The snow on the surrounding grass verge was undisturbed, except for the criss-cross marks of a sparrow, but as the boys made their way along the High Street, Charlie was looking for a different sort of track.

"He said he was going to skate on Cornhill, Have you any idea where Cornhill is?" he asked Gus.

"Somewhere in the city, I think," said Gus. "Seems a funny place to skate. I guess things were different in the old days."

"He'd better come skating back here," said Charlie. "I've things to settle with that ghost."

"Did I tell you?" asked Gus. "Mum's buying me some roller-skates for Christmas after all. I had to promise I'd only wear them in the park, though."

In the amusement park snow clung thickly to the climbing frame and the unused swings.

"I bet the pond's frozen," said Gus. "What's going on there, anyway?"

All the children in the park were gathered around the Skateopia, laughing and clapping and cheering. A now familiar figure, with a red comforter thrown across its nightshirt, was zooming up and down the half-pipe on a skateboard with blue wheels.

"Hollo! Hoop! Chirrup! Merry Christmas!" cried the figure, sailing through the air, alighting on the frozen pond and kickflipping extravagantly around the rim of it. The ghost raised its nightshirt a few inches and light seemed to issue from the calves of its legs, which shone like moons.

Narrowly missing an overhanging willow-branch, it leapt from the nose to the tail of the skateboard, deftly turned a somersault and sailed around the pond in a handstand position.

"Look out, the ice is cracking!" cried someone.

"Chirrup! Yoho! Hoop!" sang the ghost, sticking his elbows into his transparent belly and going down to a crouch.

"Keep away from the middle," yelled Charlie. The ghost took no notice of him. It was busy trying out a one-legged Daffy Duck.

In the middle of the pond a piece of ice splintered and sank, but the ghost seemed oblivious of the cries of the children. With a flick of the ankles, a cry of triumph and a final chirrup it slid into the deep, black water. There was a moment of horrified silence.

"My skateboard!" moaned Charlie. "My beautiful skateboard!"

"It's a shame you lost your skateboard," said Gus. "But what about the ghost?"

"Oh, he'll be right," said Charlie. "Ghosts can't die twice . . . can they?"

It seemed that Charlie was right. On Christmas morning, exciting parcels began to arrive for the tenants of Jubilee block, all marked with the compliments of Ebenezer Scrimp, Esquire.

Charlie, in disgrace over the loss of his skateboard, was slightly cheered to find in his parcel a big jar of striped mint sweets, but when he put one into his mouth it immediately disappeared.

Old Mrs Merritt ran upstairs clutching a huge box of violet creams with old-fashioned sugared whirls on top, but as she offered them round and people bit into them, the chocolates disappeared as well.

Mrs Ogilvie's Christmas pudding disintegrated as soon as she poured brandy over it, much to her daughter's disgust, and Gus's mother, having taken great pains to prepare the fine, fat turkey from Ebenezer Scrimp, Esquire, gave a cry of exasperation when it fell to powder under the carving knife.

"Never mind, Mum," laughed Gus, who much preferred sausages and streaky bacon, "it's only that old spook up to his tricks again. With presents it's the thought that counts."

He turned his eyes lovingly to a large cardboard box on the settee and gave a sudden cry. "My roller-skates! Mum! What's happened to my roller-skates?"

The box was empty, and cold air from an open window billowed the curtains. There was a faint "Hollo, hollo, hoop!", a ghostly snigger, and the rushing of wheels.

THE FORBIDDEN CHILD

Leon Garfield

The pleasures of youth are best remembered; those of age are best savoured as they come. So it is with Christmases. Best to forget the awful certainty that the world would end on December 24; or that for some equally cogent reason Christmas would never come, so that, when it did come, one was so over-wrought with anxiety on its behalf that one was infallibly sick and infallibly given castor oil.

Best to remember Victoria Station, where my Christmases always seemed to begin. A magical hissing cave of steam and tinsel bazaars, with nuts, grapes and oranges piled high in the fruit-shop window, like gorgeous Alps under eternal cotton-wool; and herald angels singing under the clock and shaking scarlet collecting boxes. Best to remember the bus – or, if times were good, a taxi smelling like a wallet – to an Aunt and Uncle grand in North London, with a river at the bottom of their garden and a statue of Samson modestly endeavouring to thrust aside the pillars of a rustic arch.

Best to forget that other Aunt and Uncle (mortal enemies of the first), to whom I was sometimes despatched, and who lived in tomb-like seclusion in Highbury New Park. Charity bids me to think better of them now than I did at the time. (But Charity! you weren't there!) Fancy suggests that there had once been a Christmas in that tall glum house, and that there had been holly; but its berries got frightened white and turned into the moth-balls on which I always trod when I crept out of bed in the middle of the night.

Although I was Jewish all the year round, I never really felt it till I got into that house, where the very name, Jesus, was not to be pronounced, and the New Testament was a Satanic text. My Aunt and Uncle hated Christmas and, what was worse, denied its very existence, which angered me very much as I knew it was happening at Selfridges, on the top floor. Jesus was there, very small and pink, sitting with his proud mother in a cave of holly and sand; and so was Father Christmas, in a boat. You reached this enchanted place by means of a lift, straight out of the Arabian Nights, that was operated by a lady in pale blue velvet, with beauty spots and a powdered wig. She resembled something between a female dragoon and Marie Antoinette, and had the most refined voice I have ever heard. When she said: "Going up!" it was just my soul that soared, for all earthly parts were left behind.

But of course I never went to Selfridges on those Christmases when I stayed in Highbury New Park; where I seem to remember that the curtains were always drawn, in case some hint of pagan festivity might sparkle through. Looking back on it, I must have presented a very doleful, piteous sight, imprisoned with that gloomy pair, while the world sang outside. My Uncle was a large-faced, shouting man of whom I lived in mortal terror. My Aunt, on first acquaintance, was short. She had a round face and currant eyes, like a bun; but I soon discovered it was a bun on which a tiger might well have broken its teeth. (But Charity bids me think better of them now!)

They had a garden, but no river and no Samson. It was a condemned patch of grass imprisoned by a wall on which was a thick crust of broken glass. You got to it by an iron staircase, such as prisons have. These, then, were the Christmases it is best to forget. And yet, there is one that I remember . . .

There was a woman who came to clean, a Mrs Blowser, who had been worn down over the years into something faint and shadowy in a flowered overall. No spark of joy or pleasure ever came off her; in fact, she was ideally suited to Highbury New Park. She never spoke to me, never smiled, and came and went like a ghost. She would come on Christmas Eve, and, before she left, would murmur to my Aunt (as if something unavoidable had occurred at home), that she wouldn't be coming for the next two days. No reason was given, and none was asked. My Aunt knew perfectly well that Christmas was to blame; but no word of it was ever mentioned.

I don't know whether Mrs Blowser ever nursed a sense of grievance; possibly she did. At all events, on this particular Christmas Eve, after she'd made her mysterious communication, she stared drearily at me and then said to my Aunt that she'd "take him off her hands for the afternoon, if that would be all right, ma'am". "Where to?" asked my Aunt. "To the park," said Mrs Blowser, with a sense of wretchedness altogether fitting. I knew that park. It was all railings and stern keepers, and half a dozen depressed rabbits behind bars. "Very well," said my Aunt, detecting no possible source of joyfulness in the plan.

I went with Mrs Blowser and we walked silently in the park for about half an hour; and then she said, fainting with distress: "I thought we might call on my sister-in-law what lives quite near." I said it sounded an agreeable idea, so we walked to a street of small terraced houses with dust-bins and bottles outside.

Mrs Blowser's sister-in-law's house was Number Fourteen. It was tiny – no bigger than a doll's house, it seemed to me. The ceilings were low, the walls close together, and the fireplace was of the waistcoat pocket variety, and stuffed full of fire. Mrs B's sister-in-law's house was full of children and toys and noise and the steamy smell of puddings and mince pies; it was full of candles and coloured lights and shining faces. Mrs B's sister-in-law was giving a Christmas Party. "I've brought him," said Mrs Blowser, dolefully, "Poor little soul!"

Never can I remember a Christmas like it. Never can I remember such mountains of food and such shrieking, thumping, banging and happy games! There was Charades, and Hunt the Thimble, and Blind Man's Buff and Postman's Knock. Oh how I remember an angelic girl who smelt of burnt sugar and came blushing out for a kiss when I knocked!

There was a lighted tree and a snow-storm of cards and a Christmas Crib on the sideboard. Long I gazed at it; long I gazed at the Forbidden Child, lying in a match-box, in white crepe swaddling bands, tied with a tinsel sash. And there were the Three Wise Men, travelling on horseback from the direction of a family photograph. I think they were Red Indians in private life; but were attired for the occasion in flowing Arab robes.

"I'll have to be taking him back, now," said Mrs B after what had seemed like scarcely five minutes. "Can we give him a present?" inquired the sister-in-law. (My heart rose.) "They wouldn't like it," said Mrs B. (My heart sank.) "Something small?" suggested the sister-in-law. "If he don't say nothing about it," said Mrs B. "I know what!" said the sister-in-law. "I'll give him this. He's had his eye on it ever since he come in." She went to the Crib and gave me the matchbox with the Forbidden Child. "I got another one upstairs."

Never will I forget my guilty delight as I walked back to Highbury New Park with Mrs B. "You won't say nothing to 'em," she said. I shook my head. "I'll catch it if you let on." I nodded. "What will you tell 'em then if they asks?" I pondered. "I'll think of something," I said.

My Aunt and Uncle were waiting. "You've been a long time, Mrs Blowser." "We called at my sister-in-law's, ma'am," said Mrs Blowser. "For a cup of tea."

After Mrs B had gone, my Aunt remarked that I looked flushed and that there were crumbs round my mouth; cake crumbs. "They were having a party," I mumbled, feeling it useless to deny that much. "Party? What sort of party?" demanded my Uncle in a most menacing fashion. "A birthday party," I said. "Whose birthday?" my Uncle inquired even more menacingly. "A baby's, Uncle." "What? A party for a baby? I never heard of such a thing!" "Really, Uncle, it was! On my word of honour!" And then I added, with a burst of inspiration: "It was a Jewish baby, Uncle. On my word of honour, it was!"

THE CHRISTMAS CHERRIES

Chrétien de Troyes
translated by John Hampden

In the days of King Uther Pendragon, who was King Arthur's father, there lived near Cardiff a noble knight named Sir Cleges. He was tall, good-looking and powerfully built, and he was wealthy too, for he owned many manors and farms. He spent all his money in helping others and there were many people who needed help, because the whole country was plagued by war. Many of the knights and barons fought among themselves, so that no one was safe and there was much suffering. Sir Cleges kept open house for anyone in distress, for he was the kindest, most hospitable of men, and every Christmas he gave a great feast to which he invited everyone, rich and poor, for miles around his castle. You may be quite sure that after the feast Sir Cleges gave rich gifts, gold and silver, horses and clothing, to the minstrels who had entertained his guests by telling tales, such as this which I am telling you now.

For years the good knight lived happily in this way, with his gentle wife, Dame Clarice, and his two sons, but he grew steadily poorer. Yet he was too proud to change his way of life. He sold one manor after another to pay for all this hospitality, until he had only one manor left, and this was almost too small to keep him and his family. All their followers and servants deserted them one by one and they were left alone in miserable poverty.

When Christmas came round again Sir Cleges grew very sad, thinking of the feasts he had given, and his pride was humbled at last. He wept and wrung his hands and prayed aloud to God to have pity on him.

Dame Clarice heard that cry. She came and took him in her arms and said:

"My lord, my dear love, it will not help us to mourn for the past. Let us thank God for all his gifts to us, for he has given us a great many. This is Christmas Eve, when everyone should rejoice. Come in to dinner, and let us all do our best to be happy together."

What could Sir Cleges do but smile at her? They went in to their humble meal of bread and herbs, and made merry for their sons' sake all that day.

On Christmas morning they all went to church, and Sir Cleges felt much happier. Afterwards he went alone into his little garden, where he knelt on the grass under a cherry tree, thanking God with all his heart for God's gift of poverty. As he rose to his feet he put his hand on a low bough – and stood staring in amazement. The bough, the whole tree, which had been completely bare before, was now covered with green leaves and fine ripe cherries.

"Dear God," he cried, "what miracle is this?"

Plucking a large red cherry, he put it into his mouth. It was delicious. It was the best cherry he had ever tasted. He broke off a little bough laden with fruit and hurried into the house, calling his wife:

"My dear, my dear, look at this! Our cherry tree is covered with fruit. I am afraid it's a bad omen, it means more trouble coming to us."

His wife took the bough and marvelled at it, but her heart rose.

"This is a good sign," she said. "This means better fortune for us. But whatever happens we will thank God for it." She thought for a moment. "Now let us fill a large basket with these wonderful cherries, so that tomorrow morning early you can set out for Cardiff with it, to give it to the King. He will be so astonished and pleased that he will give you a rich gift in return."

Sir Cleges kissed her and said: "I will do just as you wish."

At daybreak next morning he set out. He had not one horse left of the many which had once stood so proudly in his stables, so he had to use the poor man's pony, a strong staff, but his elder son went with him to carry the heavy basket of fruit.

When the two reached Cardiff Castle it was nearly dinner time. Sir Cleges had been away from the court for so long that no one recognized him as he was now, old and worn and wearing shabby clothes. When he and his son went in boldly at the main gate the porter stopped them at once.

"Churls," he said, "how dare you come in here! Get out, both of you, before I break your heads with my staff. Go and wait with the beggars outside."

"Good sir," replied Sir Cleges humbly, "I beg you to let me come in. I have brought a wonderful present for King Uther from the King of Heaven."

The porter lifted the lid of the basket, and as soon as he saw the cherries he had wit enough to realize that the King was likely to give a rich reward to the bringer of such a wonderful gift.

"By heaven," he said, "you shall not come into the castle unless you promise to give me a third of anything the King gives you, whether it be gold or silver."

Sir Cleges could see no hope of avoiding this, so he said reluctantly, "I promise," whereupon the porter let him and his son pass.

At the door of the great hall the usher stopped them, swinging his staff of office menacingly.

"You churls," he said, "what are you doing here? Begone at once, or I will have you beaten from head to foot."

"Good sir," answered Sir Cleges meekly, "for the love of God, do not be angry with me. I have brought the King a present from Him who created all things. See for yourself."

The boy brought the basket forward, and when the usher saw the cherries he could hardly believe his eyes.

"By St. Mary," he said, "you shall not go into the hall unless you promise to give me on your way out a third of anything which you may get."

Very sadly Sir Cleges gave his word, and he and his son made their way into the hall. It was full of lords and ladies, whose fine clothes made the poor knight look shabbier than ever. The King's stewards came striding up to him angrily.

"How dare you enter the King's hall in those rags! Get out!"

But Sir Cleges stood his ground. "I have brought the King a wonderful present," he said, "from Him who died for our salvation." He lifted the lid of the basket and the steward stared and stared.

"By St. Mary," he cried, "never in my life have I seen such a thing at Christmas. This is a marvel indeed. I will not allow you to take it to the King unless you promise to give me a third of everything that the King gives you."

Sir Cleges was so cast down that he could not answer. He told himself sadly that all his trouble would go for nothing, for those three men would take everything.

"You rascal," growled the steward, "have you lost your tongue? Give me your promise at once or I'll have you beaten and flung out of the hall."

Sighing heavily, the poor knight replied: "You shall have a third of anything which the King may give me, I promise you."

Without another word the steward led him and his son to the dais at the top of the hall, where King Uther sat in state, under a wide canopy of cloth of gold.

Sir Cleges knelt before the King and opened his basket wide, so that everyone could see the cherries, red and ripe and glistening among their fresh green leaves. A silence fell. The fine lords and ladies looked at each other and looked again at the wonderful fruit. The King leaned forward to see the better.

"Sire," said Sir Cleges, "our Saviour, Lord Jesus, has sent you these cherries by me."

"I give thanks to Him with all my heart," replied the King, "for this is a great marvel. Bring the basket here."

Sir Cleges put the basket in front of the King, who looked wonderingly at the cherries and ate two of them. "They are as delicious as they are marvellous," he said. "They shall be passed round so that everyone in this company can taste one of them, and you who brought them shall join our feast – and your son."

Sir Cleges and his son bowed low, and thanked the King, and then found humble places for themselves at one of the long trestle-tables which ran the whole length of that great hall. The King and the noblest of the court took their seats at the high table on the dais. The trumpets sounded, and the feast began. There was rich food in plenty: all kinds of meat, fish and fowl, good wine and good ale, elaborate cakes and pastries, but for everyone present the crowning wonder was a fresh, ripe red fruit. For the rest of their lives they told the story of the Christmas cherries.

When the feast was over the King said to a squire: "Ask the poor man who brought the cherries to come to me."

Sir Cleges came at once and knelt on one knee before the King.

"You have done great honour to our feast and to me," the King said, "and I will reward you gladly. I will give you anything you ask, in gold or silver, goods or lands or anything else."

"Thank you, my liege," replied Sir Cleges, "but there is only one reward I wish: your gracious permission to give twelve blows with my staff to three men in this hall."

The King looked at him in astonishment. "You make me regret that I gave you that promise," he said. "Will you change your mind, and let me give you gold or precious stones from my treasury? Do you not need money?"

"Alas," said the knight sadly, "it would be of no use to me. All I ask is twelve blows."

"Then you must have my permission to give them, because I gave you my word."

Sir Cleges and his son bowed low once again. The King rose from the table, and as soon as he had left the hall the knight looked round for the steward.

There he was, at the far end of the hall, keeping watch at the great door. Grasping his heavy staff more tightly, Sir Cleges strode towards the door, and the steward turned to meet him.

"You are to give me one-third of everything which the King gave you," he said harshly, "or I will have you whipped and take it all."

"The King gave me twelve blows," replied Sir Cleges, "and I will gladly give you your share." He swung his staff above his head. "One, two, three, four."

The steward howled with pain, and bystanders laughed, for no one liked him, and Sir Cleges went on into the antechamber. The usher came scurrying after him at once, calling out: "Churl, churl, curses on you, give me my reward."

"Gladly," replied the knight. "Here you are. Five, six, seven, eight."

He went into the courtyard, towards the main gate, and at once the porter barred his way.

"What did the King give you, churl?" asked the porter, glowering.

"Twelve strokes," the knight answered, "and you shall have your fair share. Nine, ten, eleven, twelve."

The last blow beat the porter to his knees. Leaving him to the crowd, Sir Cleges went back to the great hall, with his son still close behind him. The tables had all been cleared. A score of serving men were busy lifting them from their trestles, to be carried away, while others strewed fresh rushes on the floor.

The King was in his parlour, with a few of his lords and ladies, drinking spiced wine beside a blazing fire, while one of his court minstrels sang a lay of knightly deeds.

Sir Cleges stopped at the door and listened in amazement, for the minstrel was singing of him.

When the song was finished the King gave a gold coin to the minstrel. "Sir Cleges was a brave and worthy knight," he said. "It is years since he came to court, and I miss him sadly. Where is he now?"

"I do not know," answered the minstrel. "He has gone away from this country."

Sir Cleges came forward, bowing to the King.

"Ah," said the King, "now tell me, why did you ask only for twelve strokes?"

The knight told him the whole story, and the King and all his courtiers laughed and laughed.

"This is a noble jest!" he said at last. "Bring the steward to me." And when the steward came, still rubbing his back, the King cried, "Well, Sir Steward, you got your deserts from this poor man. What have you to say for yourself?"

"May the devil fly away with him!" roared the steward. "I'll never speak to him again!"

The King laughed again, and said to the poor knight, "What is your name?"

"Sir Cleges, sir. As I hope for salvation, I am he."

"What!" cried the King. "Are you indeed that noble knight whom I have missed for so long?"

"Indeed, sire, I am. God has brought me low, as you see, but I am Sir Cleges."

"I see now that you are," said the King, "and I welcome you with all my heart. You shall not remain in poverty. I will make you governor of this Castle of Cardiff and lord of all its lands. I will give you from my own treasury all the gold and silver that you may need, and you shall not leave me again."

"I thank you, sire," answered Sir Cleges, "and I thank God for the Christmas cherries."

THE DAY WE THREW THE SWITCH ON GEORGIE TOZER

Brian Alderson

George Tozer was one of those clean boys. They're not very common creatures, that's true but you probably know what I mean because they seem to be very evenly spread out. Every school, every block, every estate usually has a specimen: boys with unnaturally clean faces, and hair always cleaving neatly to their scalps. Some – and George was one of them – have even been known voluntarily to go with their mothers to the shops, wearing a tie and gloves, and standing one pace to the rear with a wicker basket.

George Tozer was also a good boy. At school he didn't release small rodents in Morning Assembly like Danny Price used to do, and at home he didn't kick the paintwork or slam doors like that girl Rebecca. But if you ask me, this wasn't because he made great efforts to be good; it was more because he was born that way. He just couldn't help it – and that's not really something to be proud of.

But in a perverse way George Tozer was proud of all this goodness and cleanliness, and that was where the trouble started. You see he'd cultivated a rather demure, dimply smirk, and whenever there was any strife he was liable to grin round at everybody, as much as to say: "Well, it's not my fault" and that was infuriating. The word would go round "Get Tozer!", but I must say, that when the time came, he was very good at not being got. Nobody knew a more varied selection of back ways home to escape ambush, and no one was better prepared against practical jokes ("Huh! Buttermilk Soap", he said one day when he came round to our place for tea, casting aside the stuff we'd got from the Magic Shop that's meant to cover you with slime when you wash with it).

It is my belief that George Tozer enjoyed these pranks. It made every day a kind of April-Fools-Day for him and gave him something to look forward to. It also meant that we were constantly trying to find some ingenious new way of tricking him. So it was, that at the time that I'm telling you about we had a scheme planned that we really thought would strike him to the foundations and drive that dimply grin below surface for a week or two. It was all to do with Jackson's ghost . . .

Now Jackson was my best friend — so it isn't actually his ghost I'm talking about, but the ghost that some people thought he'd got in his house. You see Jackson and his sister Jenny lived in this tall, old decrepit place, which their parents had bought for practically nothing because it was said to be haunted. Years ago a fellow had lived there whose wife had killed herself (hanged herself from the attic ceiling by her own hair, so the rumour had it) and word got about that she kept revisiting the scene of the catastrophe. The estate agents said this gave the house "historic character" but it took a family like the Jacksons to buy it.

They were far too busy to worry about ghosts. Whenever Mr Jackson was at home he climbed under a car and did things to it with grease guns, and as for Mrs Jackson she was a great one for crafts: pottery classes one week and pokerwork the next. My friend Jackson was actually more nervous than any of them. He said he'd heard slithery noises and gasps overhead when he'd been in his bedroom making a model aeroplane. But his sister Jenny, who had the pokerwork temperament, said it was nonsense and he'd been watching too many Late Nite Horror Shows!

Anyway, this was our plan for tricking old Georgie Tozer, and we thought it quite a neat one: we'd get him round to the

Jacksons' to play one afternoon (not too difficult, since his Mum was a friend of my Mum and J's Mum and they were always trying to bring Georgie's good influence to bear on us), then we decided that we'd get him up to the attic and haunt him.

I was to take him up there under the pretext of having tea, all snug and away from the grown-ups, while the other two were ostensibly going to fetch a tray-ful of things to eat. But Jackson would in fact go down to the cellar where all the electrical switches were, and Jenny would be installed in the attic, and then, at just the right moment, Jackson would throw the switch and plunge the room in darkness and Jenny would turn into the ghost of the unfortunate lady who hanged herself.

Jenny's actual ghostliness was really rather ghastly. The way we'd worked it out was this: when I brought George into the attic she would be hiding in the far corner behind the chest-of-drawers. When the light went out she would creep on to the top of this chest and peer down at Georgie with a torch shining under her chin. I don't know if you've ever tried this, but if you get the torch in the right place it gives the effect of disembodied features floating in mid-air (very horrid). What's more, Jenny had long hair, seemingly just like the woman in the story. She got hold of one of those torches with colour filters so that she could slide different strips across the bulb and turn herself blood-red or sickly-green in a very unnerving way.

We rehearsed the whole exercise over and over again. Jenny rigged up some cushioned steps on to the chest-of-drawers, so that she could get up there quickly and quietly, and she practised holding the torch so that she could get the angles right by instinct. I might say that the first few times that Jackson and I were the audience we were fairly terrified ourselves. The attic was a big one and, in the dark, you had this sense of not knowing where to go to escape this grisly face with its stringy hair.

Well – the day came for our tea-party, and George Tozer

and I went back with the Jacksons from school. It was getting towards Christmas – damp and chilly – and we were glad to flop down in front of the Jacksons' fire when we got in. We played some games and Jenny cheated dreadfully, which drew forth arguments from pernickety old George and made us feel very virtuous about putting the frights on him.

Eventually the time came for the haunting. "I'll go and see about some tea," said Jenny, and made off apparently towards the kitchen where Mrs Jackson was, I suppose, cutting sandwiches or baking cakes or something. A couple of minutes later, as arranged, Jackson suggested that we all go upstairs for our private picnic and I shepherded George along while J peeled off "to help" – or rather to get down the cellar where he could turn off the lights.

Everything had been very carefully timed with watches. We knew that it would take George and me about one minute and forty seconds to get up to the attic and park ourselves in chairs by the radiator, with George strategically placed facing Jenny's chest-of-drawers. Then we were going to leave about another half a minute for me to make some excuse and drift off out of the room where I could hold the door shut in case our victim thought to flee from the terror by night. (This wouldn't be easy though. You try escaping from a ghost in a large, pitch-black unfamiliar room with an assortment of chairs, boxes and cast-off bits of furniture all over the floor.)

The plan worked perfectly. We climbed upstairs to the attic with George apparently accepting that afternoon tea in an attic was only to be expected at the Jacksons. We settled down in the place appointed (I was dreadfully worried that Jenny would gasp or giggle or sneeze behind her chest-of-drawers, but she was as quiet as a dormant ghost ought to be) and then I muttered something about seeing where everyone was, and wandered out of the room.

Just as I closed the door behind me Jackson down in the cellar threw the switch and everything went black. The silence and suddenness of the event was alarming in itself, but I hung on to the door handle and tried to hear what was happening through the keyhole. There was a creak as soon as the light went out, which suggested that George had jumped to his feet, but he didn't seem to be moving about, and he didn't seem to be responding to Jenny who, by now, must have been starting her torch routine. There was nothing.

Then suddenly there was more than we bargained for. There was a shriek of a kind that, in that darkness, seemed to come from some caged monster – piercing, but at the same time sobbing and bubbling. It didn't happen just once. It happened again and again, and I shoved the door open to try and find out what was going on. At the same instant on came the lights again, and I saw poor old George Tozer flat on his back on the floor. He looked as though he was in some sort of fit, twitching and jerking, with his skin all blotchy grey, and white round the bottom of his cheeks. "The face . . . " he kept mumbling, "the face . . . the face . . . the face . . . "

"Don't be daft, George," I said, "it's only Jenny" – looking round to see where she'd got to. And as I did so there was a great commotion on the stairs and in burst Mrs Jackson in a frantic temper. "What the hell's going on! You had us damn near scald ourselves down there!" And there behind her, white-faced and appalled, straight from the kitchen – where she'd been made to stay and make the tea – was Jenny.

CHRISTMAS AND PETER MOSS

Mary Small

The waste ground close to the water's edge belonged to the Harbour Trust. Except for the gulls it was no good for anything.

Nearby, partly hidden by trees, stood a small stone cottage. Peter Moss lived there. Once he had been a ship's engineer and had travelled all over the world . . . a long time ago.

The cottage was old, much older than Peter Moss. His grandfather had built it back in the early days. Many times the council had tried to buy it to make way for new buildings, but it was not for sale. Peter Moss often wondered what would happen to it when he died. He had no family, only Bosun, his dog.

Every day, Peter Moss and Bosun walked down to the waste ground for exercise. Bosun was young and full of energy. He loved to chase the stones and sticks that his master threw for him. When the old man grew tired, he would stand leaning on his stick gazing across the water to the tall, skyscraper buildings of the city. Sometimes a container ship would pass on its way to the docks and there were always ferries coming and going. Peter Moss reckoned that he had the best view in the city. Yet, in spite of the bustle around him, he was lonely.

Every other day, except Sunday, Peter Moss made the long slow walk to the shops at the top of Clark Street to buy groceries. It always alarmed him to see the bulldozers busy so near to his home and more and more flats rising up to the sky, full of new people. No one took any notice of the old man; they were too busy, too worried about their own affairs.

"Christmas gets earlier and earlier every year!" Peter Moss muttered as he looked in the shop windows. It was the time of the year he dreaded the most, for he was a shy man and although he had money it could not buy him friends.

One Saturday morning he was surprised to see three youngsters with bikes walking around the waste ground talking together. They stayed there a long time and then went away.

On Sunday, more children came. They seemed very excited about something. They took spades and started to dig up the ground. Peter Moss stood at the window watching. He didn't like to interfere but they had no right to intrude. He waited a while, then opened the door and walked down with Bosun.

"What are you doing?" he asked. "This land belongs to the Harbour Trust. You can't dig it up like that."

"Why not?" said Glen, the biggest boy. "It's not used for anything."

"We need somewhere to ride our BMX bikes," said Nikos.

"The street's no good," said Werner, punching the ground with the heel of his boot.

"You'll get into big trouble if you do anything with it," said Peter Moss.

"But we want to make a practice track with dips and jumps," said Michelle. "For that we need rough ground. This couldn't be better."

All the youngsters stood and stared at him. Peter Moss didn't know what to do. "You'll have to find somewhere else," he said gruffly. Not wanting to argue, he called to Bosun and started to walk away. He could feel their strong resentment.

The youngsters muttered among themselves.

"There isn't anywhere! shouted Glen angrily.

Peter Moss stopped. The children were right; for them there

was nowhere. Youngsters nowadays didn't have the space he had when he was a boy.

"Watch it!" said Glen. "Old Nosey-Parker's coming back!" Spades in their hands, they stood and waited.

"I've just had a thought," said Peter Moss. "I'm on the Harbour Trust Board Committee. You leave the ground alone and I'll have a talk to them and maybe to the council too."

"O.K. by us," said Glen. "When will you know?"

"That I can't say," said Peter Moss. "You'll have to be patient. Come back and see me later this week. I live in the cottage up there."

The boys were at school when the people from the Harbour Trust came. They spent a long time looking at the land and a long time talking to Peter Moss. Then they went away. The old man felt sad. They hadn't made a decision one way or the other. He knew that if the children didn't get the land they'd blame it on him and go elsewhere.

"This sort of thing takes time," he said when the children knocked on the door.

Just when he had almost given up hope, the telephone rang. As Peter Moss listened to the voice a big smile spread over his face.

"The kids will be delighted," he said, "Yes, I'll be only too pleased to keep an eye on things. I'm sure there'll be no trouble."

So the children and their friends dug ditches and made jumps and a track for their BMXs.

As the days grew longer, the old man had company most evenings and all the weekends. It was impossible for him to be lonely. When they weren't riding the children would sit on the veranda and talk to him.

"When I was young they didn't make bikes like that," said Peter Moss in amazement as Werner shot out from a ditch and twisted his bike in the air, and Nikos and Glen bounced over the whoopy-doos.

"They're very expensive," said Elke. "Gino and Francesco who live next to us are selling newspapers to buy them."

"My brothers Jose and Mario are getting them for Christmas," said Rosa, "but you mustn't tell. It's a secret."

"Nikos hopes to trade his for a better one," said Sofie.

"No way can I get one," said Richard. "My dad's out of work."

"Nor me," said Paul. "We haven't the money."

From the conversations, Peter Moss was surprised that so many of the children living in the street came from different countries, places he knew quite well from his years at sea; Nikos and Sofie from Greece, Werner and Elke from Germany, Gino and Francesco from Italy, Jose, Mario and Rosa from South America, Michelle from France, Danny and Kate from England. He heard about Tuan and Khai who had come from Vietnam in an open boat.

"They live over the shop next to the Chinese restaurant," said Kate. "They seem very poor and can't speak much English."

Peter Moss started to do a lot of thinking.

The Friday before Christmas, a white panel van pulled up at his house. When it had gone, Peter Moss went up the street to the hardware store. He bought a piece of chipboard, a small tin of paint and a brush. Then he went home and locked the door. He was busy all day.

Danny was the first to notice the sign hung on the veranda.

"Look!" he said, calling to the others. "BMX BIKES FOR HIRE, NO CHARGE. Say! What has the old man done?"

Dropping their bikes, the children raced up to the cottage and banged on the door. Bosun barked as Peter Moss opened it.

"Happy Christmas!" he said. "Come in and see!"

They crowded inside and there in a little back room stood four brand new bikes.

"For anyone who needs one," said Peter Moss. "I asked for the best in the shop."

"They're sure good!" said Michelle. "Look, snake-belly tyres, chrome-moly frames and all!"

Talking excitedly, the children jostled each other to hold the bikes.

"It's unreal!" said Glen. "Gosh! Thanks a million. Wait'll we tell the others."

Next evening, the children called a meeting at Werner's and Elke's house.

"What do you think he does at Christmas time?" they said. "Probably nothing much." Excitedly their talk continued.

On Christmas Eve, Peter Moss went to the shops early to buy food for himself and Bosun. Everyone smiled at him. "Happy Christmas, Mr Moss!" they said. "Happy Christmas!" He had friends everywhere.

The waste ground lay silent and empty that evening. Peter Moss had just sat down to tea when Bosun growled softly. There was a noise of feet shuffling on the veranda, then suddenly voices started singing. Peter Moss went to the door and opened it. There stood Nikos and Sofie and all their Greek friends. Peter Moss had never heard a song so beautiful.

"Happy Christmas, Mr Moss!" sang out Rosa, and the carol singers moved aside so that her brothers Jose and Mario could carry a Christmas tree into the house. They placed it in a corner of the kitchen and the visitors crowded round, covering it with goodies and decorations.

"Our dad reckoned you'd need some good cheer," said Danny and Kate, putting a bottle of whisky under the tree.

"And I bought a new collar for Bosun," said Richard.

"And I've brought him biscuits," said Paul.

"You must eat this tonight," said Elke, placing a cake plaited and covered with icing on the table. "We call it a *stollen*. Gino and Francesco have something for you too," and the Italian boys came forward with a dish full of delicious-looking toffee.

"It's *torrone*," said Gino. "Mum made it from almonds and sugar and honey. She sends you good wishes."

Mike went to the door and pushed Tuan and Khai towards the old man. They held out a lighted lantern made from paper and smiled shyly.

"It's from their Moon Festival," said Werner. "They want you to have it."

"You're invited to dinner at our place tomorrow," said Glen and Donna. "Roast turkey, plum pudding, the lot. Did you have anything planned? We'll fetch you at midday."

"We must hurry," said Rosa, "for we have our dinner tonight after church."

"We have ours too!" said Francesco.

"And so do we!" said Elke and Sofie.

Peter Moss sat down in his chair at the table. He looked at the children and the bright things around him. There were tears in his eyes.

"Thank you," he said very softly. "It's the most wonderful Christmas I've ever had."

THE WEATHERCOCK'S CAROL

Diana Ross

On top of the cathedral was a weathercock, golden and proud. It did not look very big when you saw it from the ground, but people said it was as big as a man, and Hensel used to look up at it as he sat begging in the cathedral square and imagine himself riding on its back, flying about at midnight all over the lands and seas, and perhaps on All Hallow E'en, when anything is possible, joining in a great flight of weathercocks, a great flapping of metal wings flying for the sheer joy of flight, as he saw the lapwings doing in the high fields above the town.

Sometimes Hensel had Caterina with him and then he used to tell her all about the golden birdie, but Caterina was only just two, and though she looked very solemnly at the cathedral cock she never listened to his stories for very long, and as he never earned so much at his begging when she was with him he was not often allowed to take her.

Normally he earned a good deal, because the cathedral was famous throughout the world not only for the magnificence of its building but for the beauty of its music, and its choir was the largest and most renowned in the civilized world.

And this was only to be expected, seeing that it was sacred to St. Cecilia.

Legend had it that one day she appeared in person to a shepherd piping to his sheep in the meadows by the river, and that she had said:

"Oh, Shepherd, if you make such sweet music to draw together your sheep, will you not make music to draw together God's sheep?"

And then she had sat down on a stone, taken his pipe and played upon it, whilst the valley was filled with the music of Heaven itself. And when the vision faded the shepherd had gone home and together with his companions had built a little church on the place where the vision had come to him; and though that little church had now grown to be a vast cathedral, and the tiny hamlet of shepherds a great town, in the very centre of the magnificent altar was the very same stone, grey and rough, on which the saint had sat.

But although Hensel made his living from the pilgrims who visited the town he knew little and cared less for the reason of their coming.

He lived in a little alley which ran alongside the cathedral, so close that you could have heard the ordered sounds of the services going on within, had not the squalling of the children and the brawling of the men and women not disintegrated every other sound.

There never seemed a still or quiet moment in the alley. By day it was the children who kept the place in an uproar, but at night there was a worse and more sinister disturbance, for this alley so close to the sanctity of the great church harboured every villain and rogue that a great mediaeval city knew well how to breed. No honest man dare come here, and if the inhabitants of the alley left it to go begging, as Hensel went, that was the most innocent of their purposes.

Hensel's was the corner house and from the little window in the attic where they lived he could see the soaring pinnacles of the cathedral, the quiet sculptured saints, the spire, and even, if he lay on his back, his body half out of the window, the weathercock at the top.

He often squatted at the window with Caterina on his knee, telling her stories about the warrior saint with a chipped nose who stood opposite staring at them stonily; or throwing a few crumbs from his own meagre share to the grinning lion, who spouted water from the gutters whenever it rained; or wondering what the weathercock was looking at from his point of vantage up there. And then he did not notice the scolding and quarrelling that went on incessantly between his mother and father, his aunt and his five grown-up cousins, all of whom shared the one small attic.

Hensel was neither better nor worse than you might have supposed him to be, growing up in such surroundings.

He could hardly open his mouth without using obscene or blasphemous words: his chief concern was to get for himself as much as he could of those things he wanted, and although he wanted a great many things it was little enough he got.

Next he strove to avoid the beating which would come from anyone who happened to notice him; and then to cut a figure among the other lads of the alley with whom he fought and played, and mostly fought.

But, on the other hand, he loved his sister Caterina as well as he loved himself, and was ready to share with her any of the few good things he got by theft or good fortune. As he hated with good reason all the grown-ups with whom he came in contact, all his natural affection – and he was naturally very affectionate – was devoted to Caterina, the only one of his family who did not curse and beat him.

But as for truthfulness, honesty, cleanliness, sobriety, respect and the many virtues to be expected of a child, he knew them not nor even that he should.

Well, one day in the early spring, when it was suddenly hot almost with the heat of summer, Hensel had taken Caterina with him to the square and was sitting on the steps of the fountain.

"You have been playing enough now, Caterina," he said. "You are all hot and tired. Come and sit here beside me. Look, the golden bird shall sing you to sleep. Do you see him? Now, head in my lap and listen. 'Cock-a-doodle-do.' It's faint, I know, but then he's a long way up. But listen and you will hear. He shall sing it especially for you."

And as the little girl put her head on his knee Hensel began to sing, in a high clear voice, a song then popular in the alley, which seemed to him a nice song and quite suited to the occasion.

> *The devil is a bad man*
> *With horns upon his head,*
> *Which is the way to know him*
> *The old man said.*
> > *Cock-a-doodle-do.*

The cock-a-doodle-do was added by Hensel himself to indicate for Caterina the source of the singing.

> *The devil is a bad man*
> *With horns upon his crown,*
> *Which is the way to know him*
> *From others in the town.*
> > *Cock-a-doodle-do.*

> *The devil is a bad man*
> *With hooves upon his feet,*
> *Which is the way to know him*
> *From others that you meet.*
> > *Cock-a-doodle-do.*

"Can you hear him, Caterina? Quiet now. Lie still, he knows some more. He knows all the songs in the world and he will sing them all if you are quiet and listen."

> *The devil is a bad man*
> *A tail he has behind,*
> *Which is the way to know him*
> *From the rest of humankind.*
> > *Cock-a-doodle-do.*

> *The devil is a bad man*
> *With tail and hoof and horn,*
> *The only way to tell him*
> *From the best man born.*
> > *Cock-a-doodle-do,*
> > > *Cock-a-doodle-do.*

And the last cock-a-doodle-do went soaring up effortless and clear, higher and higher, clear and high as the soaring spire itself.

"By my faith," said a voice behind him, "that is a strange kind of lullaby with which to sing a baby to sleep! But what is your name? If you had your song of the devil you had your voice of an angel!"

Hensel had not been aware that anyone stood near him and at the unexpected sound of the man's voice he started so that Caterina nearly slipped from his lap. But she did not wake and Hensel at once began to beg, whining through his nose professionally.

"Oh, sir, I must sing my little sister to sleep for she is hungry and she cries, and I have nothing to give her and we have not eaten today nor yesterday. So I try to make her sleep and then she doesn't cry. Oh, sir, you have got a kind face, you will not let us go hungry. Give me something to buy bread. God will bless you, the saints in Heaven will bless you."

"Be quiet," said the man, who now came round in front of the boy and revealed himself as a priest. "Tell me your name and where you live and how you came by a voice like that."

Now among themselves the inhabitants of the alley might answer to their names, or at all events to the names they chose to be known by for the moment. But even the youngest children knew enough to conceal their names from strangers and to hide their dwelling place, for there were not many in the alley anxious to be generally known and found.

So now Hensel became suspicious and made as if to lift Caterina and move away.

The priest, who knew the habits of the beggars, smiled. "Ah, well!" he said. "You need not answer me now. You shall be as nameless as the nightingale in the thicket. But tell your father this. If he cares to bring you to the Choirmaster's house after vespers this evening, and anyone respectable can tell you the way, he shall get more by you hereafter than he gets from your begging now."

And the priest gave Hensel a silver coin and went on his way.

Hensel had never before held so much money in his hand, and he gloated over it, weighing it and polishing it and studying the inscription, his quick brain considering all that it promised.

If he could get it changed he could take the half of it back to his father and still escape the beating he got when he did not come home with enough money, and the other half and anything more he might earn today he could keep for himself and Caterina.

On the other hand he knew that if he went home with the silver coin intact his father would certainly pay attention to what the priest had said, which otherwise he would ignore, and Hensel was sharp enough to guess what had been in the priest's mind.

So, hard as it was for him to forego the spending of half the money, he yet decided to do so. Waking Caterina, who began to cry, he did not wait to comfort her but hurried her away across the cathedral square to the alley.

Panting, he reached the top of the attic stairs with Caterina now roaring like a lion, and his mother flew out at him and boxed his ears before he had said a word. But Hensel pushed past her and went into the room and across to where his father was brooding by the table.

"The devil seize you," cried the man. "What brings you here at this time?" And he, too, raised his hand to strike the boy.

But Hensel thrust the coin towards the father and poured out to him the tale of the stranger in the square. As he spoke his mother and cousins gathered round, each commenting after their fashion.

"Come, Kasper," said the woman. "If you take the boy who knows what good may come of it? You need not tell your name, nor where we hide. And if there is money in it 'tis a risk worth taking."

And there were murmurs of approval from the rest.

"Ah, but you be quiet," he growled, "and give a man time to think. If the priests get the boy, money there may be, but how am I to come by it unless they know where to find me?

135

And if they know where to find me the gallows may find me too. I see the trick of it."

But handling the coin he seemed to gain confidence and grudgingly at last he consented to take the boy to the rendezvous.

He need not have been afraid.

The choirmaster, for it was he who had spoken to the boy in the square, was too anxious to get him for the choir to make difficulties; and when Kasper stipulated that to compensate him for the loss of the boy's services he should be paid a monthly stipend, to be collected personally from the almoner of the monastery in which the choristers were incorporated, the priest agreed, a document to that effect was drawn up, Kasper made his mark, the priest signed, and there was Hensel delivered over to the choirmaster as if he were so much merchandise.

Now when Hensel had guessed at the priest's meaning that morning he had instantly imagined himself all dressed up in the scarlet and white robes of a chorister, leading a procession through the streets on feast days, with everyone kneeling as they passed.

He had not considered what appearing in such a procession might involve in the way of training and a changed life, and when he suddenly realized that his father was going and that he was being left alone with the priests, that he was to be separated from Caterina and the familiar life of the attic and the streets, he was suddenly seized with panic, and rushing at his father snatched at his arm, clinging to his clothing and crying:

"Don't leave me, don't leave me here. I want to come home. I want Caterina. Father, please. I don't want to stay here. I didn't know."

His father gave him a blow on the ear which knocked him to the floor.

"You'll stay here or you'll stay in hell, just as I tell you," said he, and left the room before Hensel could get up.

But now the priest came over to him and helped him up.

"Come now, Hensel," he said. "We are not a bear-pit to eat the little boys who come amongst us. You must be a brave boy and show us that you are afraid of nothing, not even of a priest. And when you are quiet I will take you to the almoner who will give you clean clothes and make you look like the fine boy you are, and then you shall come with me all round the cathedral and I will tell you the stories of all the saints, and you shall even go up the tower and come as close to your friend the weathercock as any man may, and he shall teach you better songs than those he sang to you down in the square."

For Father Bernard, the choirmaster, knew well how few boys can resist a tower, his understanding of children being at least as great as his knowledge of the laws of harmony, which may explain why his choir was the most famous in the world at that time.

Hensel, though he did not hear all that was said, felt the kindness in the priest's voice and wondered to be spoken to in such a way. "Just as if I were Caterina and he were I," he thought to himself.

So he allowed himself to be raised up, and dried his tears and put a brave face on it when he was taken through long passages and cloisters where monks were slowly pacing, to the choristers' hostel and the almoner.

Here, for the first time in all his ten years, he was bathed, new clothes were given him and shoes, which felt strange and uncomfortable to his unaccustomed feet.

But although stripped of his rags and his ten years' dirt washed away Hensel might seem a different child, you cannot so easily get rid of ten years' ill-treatment and bad example.

Hensel was willing enough to adapt himself to his new life, for he loved Father Bernard and wished to please him, and next he loved the music and wished to excel in it; and he loved the good food and clothing and the companionship of boys whose hands were not automatically turned the one against the other. But he found the discipline which went with these things very hard to bear, and his evil habits of speech and conduct were so much a part of him that it was almost impossible for him to realize he was doing wrong until he had done it.

Feeling, when he first went among them, so different from the other boys, he had taken refuge in bravado, and painted the life from which he had come as fine and adventurous, so that the others were inclined to admire and envy him, not suspecting the background of want and misery in which such a lawless life was spent; and his lively, contentious, anarchic personality leavened the group of choristers so that even the quiet and submissive seemed in some way stirred into trouble. His worst times were when he felt lonely and longed for Caterina and the timeless, untroubled days he spent with her begging in the square; when he wondered how she was getting on without him and whether she missed him or had forgotten him.

At first when he felt thus he had asked to go home for a while but being too shy to explain the reason his request had been refused.

"You are trouble enough, my son, with all the tricks you know already. We will hardly let you be off to learn a few more. If you have time to spare spend it on your knees and pray for a submissive spirit."

And cursing the old almoner under his breath Hensel had gone off to plague his depression out of himself on the others.

Often and often the seven brothers who were charged with the chorister's welfare had begged Father Bernard to be rid of him. But Father Bernard was obstinate.

"There is neither honour nor merit in saving the souls of the saved. But save this child of darkness and you shall have done a certain good thing. And, besides, there never was a voice like his and a hundred years may never see another like it. Shall we then lose this perfect instrument to the holy Cecilia for whom the best we have is not yet good enough?"

And certainly even those who were most sorely tried by Hensel's bad behaviour could not deny the wonderful beauty of his singing.

So uneasily enough his life in the choir went on and by Michaelmas he was singing the solos and the fame of the new chorister was going abroad.

Now on Christmas Eve every year the mass sung at midnight was a great musical occasion, as well as a great religious feast. For it was the custom for a mass to be specially composed each year by one of the leading contemporary composers and it was considered among them the greatest of honours to be invited to do so, and at this time the greatest number of pilgrims flocked into the town, at least as many for the sake of the music as for the sake of the services, even though these times of which I speak were more devout than our own.

And this year Hensel was told that he should take the solos.

"My son," said Father Bernard, "Father Anselm and the other fathers in the hostel have asked me to keep this honour from you, for they say it is not right that he who behaves the worst of all the boys in the choir should be the one to receive it. But I think that perhaps if you are so chosen you may try to match the excellence of your voice with a corresponding excellence of spirit."

"I will try," said Hensel, almost speechless with joy, and feeling ready to withstand every trial and temptation of the evil one – even to the point of martyrdom itself.

And he rushed away to join the others.

"There, it is just as I thought. I will lead them all, and the prince and the court and the bishop and everyone in the town will be there, and I'll tell Caterina, and she shall hear me, and how they all praise me." For singing he may have learned but not yet modesty.

But then his eyes filled with tears as he realized that Caterina would not hear him, and would not even know the honour done him. All his pleasure was soured and when he got among the other boys he began to taunt Johannes and Pietro, the two who had until now been the soloists, so that a fight began between them, with all the others scuffling and taking sides and shouting.

Now that he was a soloist he had to attend special practices which were taken by the Italian who had composed the mass this year. The Italian was a large, explosive, ridiculous man, and Hensel would bait him and pretend not to understand his broken German, or would ask him how to sing a certain part, and would then imitate the exaggerated gestures and mouthing of the man, so that the Italian would be reduced to tears of rage and would fly at Hensel, screaming at him and beating him about the head.

But always when it seemed that Hensel must be sent back into the body of the choir he would sing an aria with such divine sweetness and ease that the Italian would fall upon him and embrace him, and Hensel hardly knew which was the worse, the beatings or the embraces. But either way he enjoyed the excitement.

But as Christmas drew near the thought of Caterina grew more insistent, and Hensel worried and schemed to think of some way of getting her to the cathedral.

He knew his father came every month to draw the money agreed upon, but he was not given word with him, and anyway he knew his father would not be bothered with messages for Caterina.

So Hensel decided to go home himself to beg his mother or one of his cousins to bring the child to the Christmas mass.

But this would not be easy. He dared not ask for permission to go out for he was certain to be refused, but to go without permission would be dangerous. The choristers had a good deal of freedom within the limits of the cathedral and the monastery, but they were absolutely forbidden from going unaccompanied into the town, and although Hensel had often thought of doing so he had always decided against it as being too risky.

But now he resolved to creep from the dormitory where they all slept, to enter the cathedral from the cloisters, and to go from thence into the street, for he knew that one door, called the penitents' door, was always left open. If anyone should surprise him he would pretend to be sleep-walking.

The night he chose to do this was the second before Christmas, and it was a cold night with a full moon and a sharp wind blowing.

Hensel dressed himself before going and hoped that this would not be reckoned incompatible with sleep-walking should he be discovered, and quickly and quietly he left the sleeping boys just as he heard the watchman cry the first hour after midnight.

All went as he had planned and he was soon running on tiptoe across the nave of the cathedral.

Intent as he was upon his escape he stopped for a moment beside a pillar to gaze about the familiar place so beautifully unfamiliar in the moonlight and shadow. The candles burning before the altar and images of the saints shone like small constellations of stars in an ecclesiastical universe. Hensel stood for a moment in wonder and delight and then he quickly ran towards the penitents' door and out into the square.

This was the first time since the spring that he had known freedom, and much as he loved his new life he took a deep breath, snuffing the street smells, and feeling tempted to run around all his familiar haunts as if he were a little dog suddenly let off the chain. But the wind made him shiver, and drawing his clothes about him he hurried off towards the alley.

He ran up the stairs and stood to get his breath outside the door, listening to the familiar ugly sounds within.

His mother was singing a tipsy song, which she often did about this time of night. The eldest of his cousins was laughing hysterically and his father was laughing, too, and cursing at the same time. But these were not merry sounds and the laughter was not happy, but the precarious elation of drunkenness, and Hensel knew well just how soon it would turn into anger and violence.

He was glad however that it had not already done so, for their present state promised him some hope of success in his errand.

He opened the door cautiously, for he knew that a sudden

intruder might meet a knife thrown towards him, and as he opened it he said:

"It is I, Hensel, I have come to see you."

There was an instant silence, and Hensel in that instant saw as if in a vision of hell the life from which he had escaped.

Until this moment he had not realized how terrible it had been. As he had submitted himself to the new life of the monastery he had sloughed off the memory of the old and had only remembered Caterina and the happiness he had had with her.

But coming to it now with other eyes the horror of the scene caught him in the heart like a sudden blow.

"I came for Caterina," he heard himself saying, and although this was not what he had meant to say, hearing it he knew that it was true.

"The devil take it!" cried his father. "Here's our fine gentleman back again! If the priests have thrown you out and I lose the money I get by you, hell's teeth, you'd better be dead."

And the man struggled drunkenly to his feet.

"Oh no, it's all right, they don't know I'm here. They will never know. They have not turned me away. But please, Father, I am singing the solos in the Christmas mass, and I wanted, I thought – Caterina, if someone . . ." and looking round he saw Caterina lying asleep in a huddle on the floor alone in the patch of moonlight by the window where they used to lie together, and his voice quavered and he fell silent and afraid.

For he suddenly realized that they were all looking at him with the special hostility that the inhabitants of the alley kept for strangers, and Hensel well knew how dangerous this hostility could be. And he realized that he was indeed a stranger, and the horror and fear with which he now looked on his home was the proof of it.

"Oh! So you wanted Caterina, did you?" screamed his mother. "Well, there she is, and a fine lot of trouble I've had by her. She won't eat, she cries all the time, and does nothing she is bid, and she bites when she's beaten, and that her own

mother, yes, her own mother, the mother who bore her!"
And staggering towards the sleeping Caterina she began to
shake her viciously.

"Oh, Mother, Mother, don't! She's too little to know! It's
only because you hit her," cried Hensel, running forward.
And he put himself between the woman and the little girl
who had woken up with a cry of fear and pain, and was
looking round with a sleepy bewildered look on her tear-
stained face.

As soon as she saw Hensel her eyes widened and she began
to sob uncontrollably.

"Hensel come Caterina," she cried, "Hensel come Caterina,"
and struggling to her feet she clutched him round the waist.

Hensel lifted her up.

"It's all right, Mother," said Hensel, seeing that his mother
was too tipsy to be reasonable. "I'll take her along with me,
and she shall not bother you again."

"Bother it is! Bother here and bother there. That's all I
get, and no one to help me. Yes, you take her off with you.
You're a good boy, Hensel, the only good boy I've got. You
won't stand by and see me bitten. Bitten and bothered by the
whole wicked lot of you."

And she began to cry in self-pity.

But although Hensel had got past his mother with the
sobbing child, his father stood menacingly between him and
the door.

"Oh, no, you don't," he said. "If you go back to the brothers
with that beauty they will know you've been out, and out you
will go again and out goes the money I get by you."

"I will bring her back in a minute," lied Hensel, "I'll bring
her back when mother is asleep."

"Oh, no, you won't," cried the woman. "You'll take her and
you'll keep her, just as you said. You're a good boy, Hensel,
the only good child I've got, and they took you away from me.
The only one to care for me. But now you will take her and
keep her and be a good boy, Hensel. And you won't interfere," she shouted, turning on her husband.

And the wretched woman fell upon the man and in a drunken fury they fought together, whilst Hensel ran quickly through the door and down the dark staircase, into the cold of the moonlit alley and away as fast as he could to the cathedral square.

Caterina was heavy to carry, and she clung to him so tightly he could hardly breathe, but he dared not pause till he had crouched down with her in the shadow of the great fountain.

"Hush, Caterina," he said. "You must be quiet. If you are not quiet they will find you and take you back."

This threat silenced the baby, who clutched at Hensel's clothes, trembling, as if she would never let him go.

"It's all right, Caterina darling, I won't let them have you. I will keep you now and somehow we will manage. But quiet now, Caterina. I must think what we must do. We can't stay here, it's too cold. Look, even the golden birdie is shivering." And Hensel pointed up to the weathercock as he had so often done before on hot summer afternoons, and there it was shining in the moonlight with the stars around it pale with the brightness of the moon.

"You see," said Hensel. "Someone has filled the sky with shining crumbs, and that is for the golden bird to eat. You never saw him eat before, and that's because he's a magic bird, and only eats at midnight, and only golden crumbs are good enough for him. See, away he struts, peck here, peck there. Look, now he's after the big ones. And the moon, the moon is his bowl of water, and soon he will sip of it. It's the silver water he drinks that makes his golden voice so loud and clear."

"More," said Caterina, when he stopped, snuggling close to him as if he had never been away and as if it were quite right and natural to be sitting by the fountain telling stories in the middle of a bitter winter's night.

"No," said Hensel, hugging her tight. "No more now. I must think what to do."

And picking her up he carried her across the square to the penitents' door, and warning her to be quiet he took her in.

Out of the wind and the moonlight it seemed comparatively warm and Hensel thankfully set her down on a bench. They could not stay here long, for although the cathedral was open for those wishing to pray, a verger went round to turn out any beggars who might have come here to sleep, and he must not surprise them on his rounds.

Caterina huddled up close to him and he kept her quiet stroking her hand, but think as he would he could see no immediate way out of their difficulties.

If he took Caterina to Father Bernard, which is what he would like to do, he thought that probably they both of them would be sent back home, he for breaking out at night, and she because they would not know what to do with her. Or else she might be sent off to the nuns up on the hillside, and she would be as good as lost to him again, for they were an enclosed order, and feeling her so close, warm and confident in his lap, her small hand holding his as tightly as she could, he could not imagine sending her among strangers.

But if he kept her with him what could he do?

Dressed in his chorister's clothes he could not go far in the town without being recognized as one of them, caught and returned to the hostel, and for the first time he realized that he would now have to give up not only the clothes but also the chorister's life. The thought appalled him.

"Oh, Caterina," he murmured. "Oh, Caterina, Caterina. You just don't know what it's like." And his throat tightened and he wanted to cry and couldn't.

Caterina did not understand him but she felt something was wrong, and came closer to placate him, and in a doubtful voice said:

"Caterina good girl."

Hensel hugged her. "Yes, Caterina good girl," and sighing heavily he picked her up again.

For he had remembered that when Father Bernard had taken him round the cathedral on that first day, and true to his promise had taken him on to the roof so that he might gaze at the golden bird, that they had gone up a small turret stairway, past the belfry loft, past other little doors and openings which led he knew not where, until they had come to a tiny room at the top from which a door led on to the roof.

To this small chamber he now resolved to go, for he was pretty certain no one would be going up there in the winter and there he would have more time to think out some plan.

Very cautiously, for fear of the watchman surprising them, he crept with Caterina to the foot of the turret stair, and then, hitching her on his back, he began to climb.

Many times he had to set her down and he even put her to climb herself, but she took so long and made so much noise stumbling on the steep stairs in the darkness that in the end he carried her once more, and he was almost exhausted when at last they reached their sanctuary.

It was terribly cold up there, for although a slit window through the thick stone wall let in a sharp needle of moonlight it also let in the biting wind. But so relieved was Hensel to get there, that he dumped Caterina down on the floor and crouched beside her almost as if he were a wanderer at last come home.

"Sleep now, Caterina," he said, "and while you are asleep I will think what to do."

But Caterina would not sleep and so Hensel began to talk over his troubles with her, almost as if she really could help him with her advice.

"The trouble is, Caterina," he said, "that I shall have to get new clothes, and how to do that without being seen is going to be difficult. Once we have new clothes we will go off, Caterina, we will take to the road and follow the pilgrims as they go to their homes. We will follow them to the south, through the high mountains, mountains all covered with snow and green ice and forests. And then we go down from the mountains into Italy, a country that is golden and sunny and warm; even in the winter it is like the springtime here. Father Bernard tells us all about these things and some of the other boys come from there." And Hensel felt the tears come to his eyes as he thought that it would probably be Pietro who would now take his place in the Christmas mass.

"Caterina go walk," said Caterina, breaking his silence.

"Oh yes," went on Hensel. "We will walk and walk, and at last we will come to Rome, a great city, far greater than this, with marble palaces in every street, and the Holy Father lives in the finest, and there he receives the pilgrims and forgives them their sins, and we will see him, too; and the pilgrims come there at every time of the year, not just once or twice at feast times as they do here, and a beggar can live there like a rich merchant lives here. And we will beg together, Caterina, and oh, what a lot we will get between us; and when we are rich and grown up we will buy a little farm. Do you remember that day in the summer when I carried you all the way up the valley to the waterfall? And do you remember the little farm on the hillside, with a pretty red cow, and the huge old pig and all the black little piglings, and they made you laugh? But you were only tiny then. But we will buy just such a farm, and I will be the farmer and you shall look after the house. And we'll keep a lot of geese and goslings and ducks and hens and a big cock, too, to remind us of the golden cock up yonder. And then we will talk of these times in the evening, and we'll wonder about them and we won't remember anything but the times you and I went begging in the square and sang to the old golden birdie. And one day when we are begging, perhaps Father Bernard will be there on a pilgrimage or visiting the Holy Father on some matter of business, and he will see us there, and after so long I will tell him why I had to run away, and then he won't be cross with me, and the Bishop won't punish me, and perhaps I might sing in a choir in Rome, and the Holy Father himself might hear me."

And so he went on consoling himself for all that he was losing now with dreams of all that should come to them in the future.

But at last Caterina fell asleep, and Hensel, too, for although you might find it difficult to sleep on a stone floor without cover, and that in the middle of winter, this was not the first time these children had been compelled to do so.

They were roused suddenly whilst it was yet dark. The whole tower shook and roared, they might have been in the heart of a hurricane. Hensel, after the first shock of waking, realized that the bells were ringing in the belfry below, and he tried to tell Caterina what it was, but as loud as he shouted not a sound could he make; he could only hold her desperate body close to his.

At last, as suddenly as it began, the ringing stopped, and Hensel found himself trembling and panting as if he had been battling with the elements. Caterina was screaming with all her might, but after the clangour of the bells it sounded a puny, unreal sound like a noise in a dream.

"Hush, hush," said Hensel. "Don't make so much noise, Caterina. The big bells will hear you, and it will make them angry and then they really will make a noise! It was only the bells, Caterina, you know, the big bells who go ding-dong. We heard them down in the square, but there they sounded gentle and polite. 'Ding-dong time to go home. Ding-dong time to be out.' It's only being so close to them makes the sound so big and fierce. It's only the bells singing to the golden birdie. The bells won't hurt you, Caterina."

And gradually Hensel calmed her and they poked their heads out of the stone window to see how nearly it was morning.

As soon as people should be about Hensel had resolved to creep out into the streets to see if he could waylay some lad and rob him of his clothing.

"I will give him these clothes of mine, and they will be better than his," he thought. "So it will hardly be robbery, and they will not get him into trouble as they would get me."

For poor Hensel now was a fair hotch-potch of morality and immorality. In the old days he had robbed as if it were the most proper thing to do in the world, and he had no idea that it was wrong, only that it was dangerous. But now, after his schooling with Father Bernard, his life was complicated like Adam's before him, with a knowledge of good and evil, and his desire to be good and to be thought good was continuously at odds with his lawless impulses; and he tried, like others before him, to justify to himself what he knew to be wrong.

He had meant to leave Caterina in the safety of the tower for, saddled with her, his task was bound to be more difficult, and even the labour of getting her up and down the immense staircase was a formidable undertaking. But knowing that the bells would probably ring again before long he could not decide to leave her alone with her terror, so take her with him he must.

Although it was slow he let Caterina scramble down the steps herself most of the time, for used to having his meals regularly he was now ravenous for his breakfast, and he decided to steal some food as well as clothing if he got the chance.

But as they reached the last twist of the spiral staircase he heard footsteps in the aisle below. Thrusting Caterina into a sitting position he shook his finger before her lips to keep her silent.

"Here we are," said a deep man's voice. "Now which are the keys of this one? Yes, here they are. These are they. So."

"But why are you locking everything up?" said a boy's voice.

"Because of the crowds who will be coming to the service tonight," said the man. "I have known people to climb up the stairway and crowd along the triforium and even up the clerestory, and although, Heaven be praised, there has never yet been an accident the Bishop has decided to take no chances, and all places but those authorized are to be locked for the festival. There."

And the children heard the heavy door shut to and the key turn in the lock, and the fainter voice of the man saying·

"Well, now to the vaults."

As soon as they were gone, Hensel turned to Caterina. "Well," said he, "That's that for you and me. Back we go, Caterina. No starting for Rome today, and no breakfast either."

And hoisting the child up he began the long climb back to the top.

It was a long dreary day they had up there. Caterina was

more used to going without food now than Hensel so he suffered the most, but she was thirsty and cried for a drink. So with some difficulty Hensel unbolted the little door which led on to the roof, and as the biting wind had now brought rain Hensel was able to scoop up water from the gutters with his hands, but Caterina like any little animal put her face down to the water and sucked it up.

Caterina wanted to walk about the roof, to make the closer acquaintance of the carved kings and queens who looked less dignified and unapproachable with raindrops hanging from the tips of their noses as if they all had colds and not a handkerchief between them. And she begged to go and see the golden birdie close, too.

But Hensel was cold enough already, without getting wet as well, so he hurried Caterina back into the tower, telling her that if she were good the golden bird would lay them a golden egg for their breakfast, cock or no cock; but if they bothered him, away he would fly and the cathedral would stand without a weathercock and no one in the whole town would know which way the winds blew.

It was really the golden bird who got them through the day, for Hensel told tales of him and sang songs about him till it almost seemed as if he himself were there to keep them company. But towards the evening even the weathercock's magic failed and Caterina grew fractious and difficult and began to whine for food. Hensel, who was himself so hungry he wanted to cry, got cross with her and scolded her, so that she cried the more and as the dusk deepened she grew so impossible to manage poor Hensel was beside himself with desperation.

"Oh, plague take it!" he cried. "I wish I had left you where you were! I shouldn't be up here starving like a fool. I'd be away down there with the others, and tonight I'd be singing to the prince and the bishop, and everyone in the town talking about me, and a fine feast afterwards. And now that fool Pietro is taking my place and grinning all over his silly face, and the greater fool I."

And he ran a little way down the stair to escape from her crying. But her sudden shriek of terror so softened him he came back to her and taking her in his arms he tried to comfort her.

"Oh, I didn't mean it, Caterina!" he said. "But sleep now, and be a good girl. If you go to sleep now I will give you a surprise. When the bells ring at midnight we will go down the stairs and listen to the singing from the little passage above the arches. No one will see us there and I will watch out so that you do not fall. And you'll see the altar all shining with candles as bright as the stars we saw last night, and the priests all in their silver and scarlet and the choirboys, too. Oh Caterina, how I wish you could have seen me in my vestments."

Caterina grew quiet as he talked, so he went on saying whatever came into his head, and, light-headed with hunger, anxiety and disappointment, a lot of nonsense he talked too.

"Just beside the altar is the figure of our blessed Saint Cecilia, and today she will wear a crown on her head, and the jewelled robes they only bring out at Christmas. I have never seen them but they say even the empress has nothing finer. And there, too, is the crib where the holy baby Jesus lies with Mary at his side and Joseph, and the shepherds and the kings; and all carved out of wood, but as big as real people. Just think of that! And a wooden ox and a wooden ass, just the same as we might have on our farm, Caterina. And on Christmas night the animals say their prayers: the cows and the horses and the cocks and the hens. Yes, even the fine old cock up yonder. For soon he will fly down to the cradle, and down he will fall on his knees, for cocks have knees on Christmas night, and 'Cock-a-doodle-do! Here I am, my master!' And he sings to Jesus at midnight the song he sings for the sun in the morning; for being a cock he can't exactly say his prayers. And all this we will see. But now you must sleep or you will be too tired when the time comes."

And looking closer Hensel saw that she had indeed fallen to sleep, and not daring to move lest he wake her he too drifted off into an uneasy dozing.

All too soon the bells awoke them and this time Hensel did not try to comfort Caterina, he picked her up and began to carry her down the stairs. As they went by the belfry loft the noise was so stupendous it seemed as if they were to pass through a den of raging monsters, and even Hensel hesitated whether to continue in his purpose. But as he paused, Caterina began to struggle so fiercely that he thought he would be able to do nothing with her if he went back, so gripping her yet more tightly he fled by the door which contained the plunging bells and down and away he went as fast as he could.

When he came to the narrow arch which led from the turret on to the ledge of the triforium, already the sound of the bells was remote and within reason. He sat on the steps till Caterina should stop crying; and seeing the soft light shining through the arch from the church beyond, curiosity soon got the better of her and she said, "Caterina good girl now," and wiped her face on Hensel's garment.

He lifted her and edged cautiously along the ledge until they had gained the first arch. There was just room for them to sit beside it, their legs tucked under them, gazing at the scene below.

Innumerable candles lit the great church, and the children could see how the prince and princess and all the court in their brilliant clothing were gathered just below them. Beyond in the nave the crowding people were so close that those still trying to enter caused a ripple in the throng as if they were stones falling into water.

On their left were the choir and the high altar, and beside it the figure of the saint enigmatically smiling and the carved crib of lifelike figures, all just as Hensel had said.

Little Caterina might have thought herself dreaming, only never, even in dreams, had she seen anything so coloured and magnificent.

She clutched Hensel's hand and pointed at the people in the nave and then at the altar blazing with candles.

"All the people," she said; "and the fire. Pretty. Caterina cook her dinner."

152

"No, no," said Hensel laughing. "Those fires will not cook you a dinner. We must wait for that, and a long time too, until tomorrow evening as like as not. But don't mind about that now, Caterina. Just look at all the pretty people, and when the music starts be a good girl and keep quiet."

As he spoke the bells above gave a final peal and were quiet, and at once the organ began to play, the music merging into itself the rustling and whispering of the crowd, and then a great hush fell on the church and only the music was heard.

At the same time a procession appeared from the cloisters, the bishop at the head, the officiating priests behind, the abbot, the cathedral dignitaries and the choristers carrying jewelled banners and candles as thick as a man's wrist.

Chanting, the procession moved round the great church so that the sound of their singing was now near now far, until they passed below the children and filed into their places at the altar and in the choir.

Hensel watched the scene as if he were two people. This was the first great festival he had witnessed, and his love of the grandeur and beauty both of sight and sound held one part of him purely enraptured. But at another level he was bitterly torn with envy and he wanted to shout out and spoil it in some way, for there he saw Pietro standing in the place that should have been his, and he heard Pietro's voice soaring serenely up like a bird flying suddenly up from a flock of its fellows.

"Oh, Caterina," he murmured, "I wish it were me. Oh, I wish it were me. I'd sing and I'd sing. Why, the old cock up there would be able to hear me, even Saint Cecilia way up in the sky. Oh, Caterina, you never did hear me sing in here where the echo makes it sound like . . . like as if the sound weren't even mine."

But as the service began Hensel forgot himself and everything but the beauty, though it seemed odd to him that the lights on the altar seemed to blaze up suddenly and then shake and blur as if they were burning under water, and he did not understand why the singing suddenly roared in his ears so that his head swam.

153

And then came the moment he had most dreamed of when preparing himself for the mass. The first of the Christmas carols was sung by a single boy's voice with the choir joining in only for the chorus. It was a lullaby, and the Italian had composed it with Hensel in mind, for it began with three "lullays" rising and rising to a clear soft note, unimaginably high, which Hensel could take with such ease that it sounded as effortless as a bird's note. But Pietro, sweetly as he could sing, was quite unable to reach it. Hensel listened grimly as the boy's voice rang out:

Lullay. Lullay. Lullay.

But sure enough Pietro's voice grated, squeaked and broke. In the moment of tense silence which followed the word was completed and then a shaky child's voice was heard to cry:

"Listen! It must go up, up, up! Up to the old golden bird up above us! Listen, all of you. I can sing you a carol, a better one than that, a carol he taught me, the golden bird, a carol you never heard before. He taught it me last night, or the night before, or just now. Or some time. Listen, it goes like this."

Vergers were hurrying to the door of the turret, for they saw how the boy swayed on the narrow ledge, holding uncertainly to the pillar, with a tiny girl crouching at his feet.

But before they could reach the turret door to unlock it and before the murmuring of the people could rise to a tumult, a strange thing happened.

"Cock-a-doodle-do," sang the boy. "Cock-a-doodle-do."

And from high, high up, as if coming from the stars, all could hear a golden voice replying: "Cock-a-doodle-do."

Hensel laughed with joy, and there came from none knew where a rush of gold, and a great shining bird hovered above the altar and alighted on the canopy and flapped its glowing wings and arched its neck, and all could see how the carved saint herself turned towards it and smiled and took the flute in her hand and set it to her lips, and the figures in the great east window came to coloured life, and the shepherds and saints and angels struck a chord upon their various harps,

lutes, organs, trumpets, dulcimers, viols and bells as Hensel
began to sing:

> *There stands a tree upon a hill*
> *That time shall not decay,*
> *And there the little birds sing so shrill*
> *That welcome in the day,*
> *So hush my little one, hush my pretty one*
> *Heed what I do say;*
> *And you shall hear how the little birds sing*
> *That welcome in the day.*

And every carved and painted saint, the stone kings and
queens, the apostles and angels, standing in every niche and
pinnacle of the cathedral within and without, took up the
chorus and played and sang while the great golden cock
flapped its golden wings and crowed.

> *There is a flower upon the tree*
> *Set fast in thicket and thorn,*
> *It is the flower of Galilee*
> *To Mary the maiden born.*
> *So hush my little one, hush my pretty one*
> *Heed what I do say:*
> *And you shall hear how the little birds sing*
> *That welcome in the day.*
> > *Lullay – Lullay – Lullay.*

And with a triumphant cock-a-doodle-do and the beating of
huge wings, the golden bird took flight, the carved saints were
still, the miraculous music was done.

Hensel heard the rush of wings and nothing more, for he
fell unconscious.

Some say an angel appeared and held him from falling off
the ledge. Some say little Caterina performed this service.

At all events, the next thing he knew he was lying in a bed
in a grand room he had never seen before, and beside him
stood the prince and princess, the bishop and other people he
did not know, and Father Bernard close to him, and crowding

155

in the room were a murmuring throng of people, courtiers, monks and priests.

"Where is Caterina?" he asked. "Where am I? Oh, Father," he said, turning to Father Bernard. "I am sorry for what I did. Will they punish me? Will they send me away? I meant no harm, indeed I didn't. But suddenly I saw such strange things."

As he spoke all in the room knelt down.

"My son," said Father Bernard, "if you did wrong you are forgiven as all of us here need forgiveness. Through you a great wonder was done this night."

"But Caterina?" he asked.

"She is here," said Father Bernard, and he raised Hensel up so that he could see how Caterina sat on the knees of a woman in a silk dress and was being fed with soup from a bowl.

"I am hungry, too," said Hensel, and burst into tears.

"Come, it is time we went," said the bishop. "The child is overcome."

And the prince, the bishop and all the great lords and ladies made the sign of the cross and rose from their knees and went quietly from the room.

Well, the end of it was that Hensel was back with Father Bernard in the choir school, and Caterina was brought up by the prince's sister to become a young lady of the court. And Hensel was able to see her whenever he wished by special dispensation from the abbot.

And whether it was the influence of the vision or that now for the first time in his life he was completely happy I don't know. But although as lively and mischievous as ever Hensel had quite lost the perversity and aggressiveness which before had made him such a plague both to others and himself.

And when, in time, his voice broke and he could be a chorister no longer, he began to study music with Father Bernard and the other great musicians of the time, so that he became in his turn master of the choir, and one of the greatest servants of his patroness, Saint Cecilia.

And the fame of that Christmas marvel was spread\abroad

through all countries, so that on Christmas Eve the pilgrims who came flocking were as numberless as the stars on a frosty night. And many diseased and afflicted came, more especially the deaf and dumb, for many of these would be cured if they should kneel through the singing of the weathercock's carol.

For thus was it known, and still is, for every Christmas ever since that time the carol has been sung, and some say that even now the great cock on the top of the spire arches its neck to the stars and flaps its wings and crows when the faint sound of the carol comes up to it from below.

But whether that is so or not I cannot say. You must go and see for yourselves.

THE THIEVES WHO COULDN'T HELP SNEEZING

Thomas Hardy

Many years ago, when oak trees now past their prime were about as large as elderly gentlemen's walking-sticks, there lived in Wessex a yeoman's son, whose name was Hubert. He was about fourteen years of age, and was as remarkable for his candour and lightness of heart as for his physical courage, of which, indeed, he was a little vain.

One cold Christmas Eve his father, having no other help at hand, sent him on an important errand to a small town several miles from home. He travelled on horseback, and was detained by the business till a late hour of the evening. At last, however, it was completed; he returned to the inn, the horse was saddled, and he started on his way. His journey homeward lay through the Vale of Blackmore, a fertile but somewhat lonely district, with heavy clay roads and crooked lanes. In those days, too, a great part of it was thickly wooded.

It must have been about nine o'clock when, riding along amid the overhanging trees upon his stout-legged cob, Jerry, and singing a Christmas carol, to be in harmony with the season, Hubert fancied that he heard a noise among the boughs. This recalled to his mind that the spot he was traversing bore an evil name. Men had been waylaid there. He looked at Jerry, and wished he had been of any other colour than light grey; for on this account the docile animal's form was visible even here in the dense shade. "What do I care?"

he said aloud, after a few minutes of reflection. "Jerry's legs are too nimble to allow any highwayman to come near me."

"Ha! Ha! indeed," was said in a deep voice; and the next moment a man darted from the thicket on his right hand, another man from the thicket on his left hand, and another from a tree-trunk a few yards ahead. Hubert's bridle was seized, he was pulled from his horse, and although he struck out with all his might, as a brave boy would naturally do, he was overpowered. His arms were tied behind him, his legs bound tightly together, and he was thrown into a ditch. The robbers, whose faces he could now dimly perceive to be artificially blackened, at once departed, leading off the horse.

As soon as Hubert had a little recovered himself, he found that by great exertion he was able to extricate his legs from the cord; but, in spite of every endeavour, his arms remained bound as fast as before. All, therefore, that he could do was to rise to his feet and proceed on his way with his arms behind him, and trust to chance for getting them unfastened. He knew that it would be impossible to reach home on foot that night, and in such a condition; but he walked on. Owing to the confusion which this attack caused in his brain, he lost his way, and would have been inclined to lie down and rest till morning among the dead leaves had he not known the danger of sleeping without wrappers in a frost so severe. So he wandered farther onwards, his arms wrung and numbed by the cord which pinioned him, and his heart aching for the loss of poor Jerry, who never had been known to kick, or bite, or show a single vicious habit. He was not a little glad when he discerned through the trees a distant light. Towards this he made his way, and presently found himself in front of a large mansion with flanking wings, gables, and towers, the battlements and chimneys showing their shapes against the stars.

All was silent; but the door stood wide open, it being from this door that the light shone which had attracted him. On entering he found himself in a vast apartment arranged as a dining-hall, and brilliantly illuminated. The walls were covered with a great deal of dark wainscoting, formed into moulded panels, carvings, closet-doors, and the usual fittings of a house of that kind. But what drew his attention most was the large table in the midst of the hall, upon which was spread a sumptuous supper, as yet untouched. Chairs were placed around, and it appeared as if something had occurred to interrupt the meal just at the time when all were ready to begin.

Even had Hubert been so inclined, he could not have eaten in his helpless state, unless by dipping his mouth into the dishes, like a pig or cow. He wished first to obtain assistance; and was about to penetrate farther into the house for that purpose when he heard hasty footsteps in the porch and the words, "Be quick!" uttered in the deep voice which had reached him when he was dragged from the horse. There was only just time for him to dart under the table before three men entered the dining-hall. Peeping from beneath the hanging edges of the tablecloth, he perceived that their faces, too, were blackened, which at once removed any doubts he may have felt that these were the same thieves.

"Now, then," said the first – the man with the deep voice – "let us hide ourselves. They will all be back again in a minute. That was a good trick to get them out of the house – eh?"

"Yes. You well imitated the cries of a man in distress," said the second.

"Excellently," said the third.

"But they will soon find out that it was a false alarm. Come, where shall we hide? It must be some place we can stay in for two or three hours, till all are in bed and asleep. Ah! I have it. Come this way! I have learnt that the farther cupboard is not opened once in a twelve-month; it will serve our purpose exactly."

The speaker advanced into a corridor which led from the hall. Creeping a little farther forward, Hubert could discern that the cupboard stood at the end, facing the dining-hall. The thieves entered it, and closed the door. Hardly breathing, Hubert glided forward, to learn a little more of their intention, if possible; and, coming close, he could hear the robbers whispering about the different rooms where the jewels, plate, and other valuables of the house were kept, which they plainly meant to steal.

They had not been long in hiding when a gay chattering of ladies and gentlemen was audible on the terrace without. Hubert felt that it would not do to be caught prowling about the house, unless he wished to be taken for a robber himself, and stood in a dark corner of the porch, where he could see everything without being himself seen. In a moment or two a whole troop of personages came gliding past him into the house. There were an elderly gentleman and lady, eight or nine young ladies, as many young men, besides half a dozen menservants and maids. The mansion had apparently been quite emptied of its occupants.

"Now, children and young people, we will resume our meal," said the old gentleman. "What the noise could have been I cannot understand. I never felt so certain in my life that there was a person being murdered outside my door."

Then the ladies began saying how frightened they had been, and how they had expected an adventure, and how it had ended in nothing after all.

"Wait a while," said Hubert to himself. "You'll have adventure enough by and by, ladies."

It appeared that the young men and women were married sons and daughters of the old couple, who had come that day to spend Christmas with their parents.

The door was then closed, Hubert being left outside in the porch. He thought this a proper moment for asking their assistance; and, since he was unable to knock with his hands, began boldly to kick the door.

"Hullo! What disturbance are you making here?" said a footman who opened it; and, seizing Hubert by the shoulder, he pulled him into the dining-hall. "Here's a strange boy I have found making a noise in the porch, Sir Simon."

Everybody turned.

"Bring him forward," said Sir Simon, the old gentleman before mentioned. "What were you doing there, my boy?"

"Why, his arms are tied!" said one of the ladies.

"Poor fellow!" said another.

Hubert at once began to explain that he had been waylaid on his journey home, robbed of his horse, and mercilessly left in this condition by the thieves.

"Only to think of it!" exclaimed Sir Simon.

"That's a likely story," said one of the gentlemen-guests, incredulously.

"Doubtful, hey?" asked Sir Simon.

"Perhaps he's a robber himself," suggested a lady.

"There is a curiously wild wicked look about him, certainly, now that I examine him closely," said the old mother.

Hubert blushed with shame; and, instead of continuing his story, and relating that robbers were concealed in the house, he doggedly held his tongue, and half resolved to let them find out their danger for themselves.

"Well, untie him," said Sir Simon. "Come, since it is Christmas Eve, we'll treat him well. Here, my lad; sit down in that empty seat at the bottom of the table, and make as good as meal as you can. When you have had your fill we will listen to more particulars of your story."

The feast then proceeded; and Hubert, now at liberty, was not at all sorry to join in. The more they ate and drank the merrier did the company become; the wine flowed freely, the logs flared up the chimney, the ladies laughed at the gentlemen's stories; in short, all went as noisily and as happily as a Christmas gathering in old times possibly could do.

Hubert, in spite of his hurt feelings at their doubts of his honesty, could not help being warmed both in mind and in body by the good cheer, the scene, and the example of hilarity set by his neighbours. At last he laughed as heartily at their stories and repartees as the old Baronet, Sir Simon, himself. When the meal was almost over one of the sons, who had drunk a little too much wine, after the manner of men in that century, said to Hubert, 'Well my boy, how are you? Can you take a pinch of snuff?" He held out one of the snuff-boxes which were then becoming common among young and old throughout the country.

"Thank you," said Hubert, accepting a pinch.

"Tell the ladies who you are, what you are made of, and what you can do," the young man continued, slapping Hubert upon the shoulder.

"Certainly," said our hero, drawing himself up, and thinking it best to put a bold face on the matter. "I am a travelling magician."

"Indeed!"

"What shall we hear next?"

"Can you call up spirits from the vasty deep, young wizard?"

"I can conjure up a tempest in a cupboard," Hubert replied.

"Ha-ha!" said the old Baronet, pleasantly rubbing his hands. "We must see this performance. Girls, don't go away: here's something to be seen."

"Not dangerous, I hope?" said the old lady.

Hubert rose from the table. "Hand me your snuff-box, please," he said to the young man who had made free with him. "And now," he continued, "without the least noise, follow me. If any of you speak it will break the spell."

They promised obedience. He entered the corridor, and, taking off his shoes, went on tiptoe to the cupboard door, the guests advancing in a silent group at a little distance behind him. Hubert next placed a stool in front of the door, and, by standing upon it, was tall enough to reach the top. He then, just as noiselessly, poured all the snuff from the box along the upper edge of the door, and, with a few short puffs of breath, blew the snuff through the chink into the interior of the cupboard. He held up his finger to the assembly, that they might be silent.

"Dear me, what's that?" said the old lady, after a minute or two had elapsed.

A suppressed sneeze had come from inside the cupboard. Hubert held up his finger again.

"How very singular," whispered Sir Simon. "This is most interesting."

Hubert took advantage of the moment to gently slide the bolt of the cupboard into its place. "More snuff," he said, calmly.

"More snuff," said Sir Simon. Two or three gentlemen passed their boxes, and the contents were blown in at the top of the cupboard. Another sneeze, not quite so well suppressed as the first, was heard: then another, which seemed to say that it would not be suppressed under any circumstances whatever. At length there arose a perfect storm of sneezes.

"Excellent, excellent for one so young!" said Sir Simon. "I am much interested in this trick of throwing the voice — called, I believe, ventriloquism."

"More snuff," said Hubert.

"More snuff," said Sir Simon. Sir Simon's man brought a large jar of the best scented Scotch.

Hubert once more charged the upper chink of the cupboard, and blew the snuff into the interior, as before. Again he charged, and again, emptying the whole contents of the jar. The tumult of sneezes became really extraordinary to listen to — there was no cessation. It was like wind, rain, and sea battling in a hurricane.

"I believe there are men inside, and that it is no trick at all!" exclaimed Sir Simon, the truth flashing on him.

"There are," said Hubert. "They are come to rob the house; and they are the same who stole my horse."

The sneezes changed to spasmodic groans. One of the thieves, hearing Hubert's voice, cried, "Oh! mercy! mercy! let us out of this!"

"Where's my horse?" cried Hubert.

"Tied to the tree in the hollow behind Short's Gibbet. Mercy! Mercy! let us out, or we shall die of suffocation!"

All the Christmas guests now perceived that this was no longer sport, but serious earnest. Guns and cudgels were procured; all the menservants were called in, and arranged in position outside the cupboard. At a signal Hubert withdrew the bolt, and stood on the defensive. But the three robbers, far from attacking them, were found crouching in the corner, gasping for breath. They made no resistance; and, being pinioned, were placed in an outhouse till the morning.

Hubert now gave the remainder of his story to the assembled company, and was profusely thanked for the services he had rendered. Sir Simon pressed him to stay over the night, and accept the use of the best bedroom the house afforded, which had been occupied by Queen Elizabeth and King Charles successively when on their visits to this part of the country. But Hubert declined, being anxious to find his horse Jerry, and to test the truth of the robbers' statements concerning him.

Several of the guests accompanied Hubert to the spot behind the gibbet, alluded to by the thieves as where Jerry was hidden. When they reached the knoll and looked over, behold! there the horse stood, uninjured, and quite unconcerned. At sight of Hubert he neighed joyfully: and nothing could exceed Hubert's gladness at finding him. He mounted, wished his friends "Good night!" and cantered off in the direction they pointed out, reaching home safely about four o'clock in the morning.

THE GIFT OF THE MAGI

O. Henry

One dollar and eighty-seven cents. That was all. And sixty cents of it was in pennies. Pennies saved one and two at a time by bulldozing the grocer and the vegetable man and the butcher until one's cheeks burned with the silent imputation of parsimony that such close dealing implied. Three times Della counted it. One dollar and eighty-seven cents. And the next day would be Christmas.

There was clearly nothing to do but flop down on the shabby little couch and howl. So Della did it. Which instigates the moral reflection that life is made up of sobs, sniffles, and smiles, with sniffles predominating.

Whilst the mistress of the home is gradually subsiding from the first stage to the second, take a look at the home. A furnished flat at eight dollars per week. It did not exactly beggar description, but it certainly had that word on the lookout for the mendicancy squad.

In the vestibule below was a letter-box into which no letter would go, and an electric button from which no mortal finger could coax a ring. Also appertaining thereunto was a card bearing the name "Mr James Dillingham Young."

The "Dillingham" had been flung to the breeze during a former period of prosperity when its possessor was being paid thirty dollars per week. Now, when the income was shrunk to twenty dollars, the letters of "Dillingham" looked blurred, as though they were thinking seriously of contracting to a modest and unassuming D. But whenever, Mr James Dillingham Young came home and reached his flat above he was called "Jim" and greatly hugged by Mrs James Dillingham Young, already introduced to you as Della. Which is all very good.

Della finished her cry and attended to her cheeks with a powder puff. She stood by the window and looked out dully at a grey cat walking a grey fence in a grey back yard. Tomorrow would be Christmas Day, and she had only $1.87 with which to buy Jim a present. She had been saving every penny she could for months, with this result. Twenty dollars a week doesn't go far. Expenses had been greater than she had calculated. They always are. Only $1.87 to buy a present for Jim. Her Jim. Many a happy hour she had spent planning for something nice for him. Something fine and rare and sterling – something just a little bit near to being worthy of the honour of being owned by Jim.

There was a pier glass between the windows of the room. Perhaps you have seen a pier glass in an eight-dollar flat. A very thin and very agile person may, by observing his reflection in a rapid sequence of longitudinal strips, obtain a fairly accurate conception of his looks. Della, being slender, had mastered the art.

Suddenly she whirled from the window and stood before the glass. Her eyes were shining brilliantly, but her face had lost its colour within twenty seconds. Rapidly she pulled down her hair and let it fall to its full length.

Now, there were two possessions of the James Dillingham Youngs in which they both took a mighty pride. One was Jim's gold watch that had been his father's and his grandfather's. The other was Della's hair. Had the Queen of Sheba lived in the flat across the airshaft, Della would have let her hair hang out the window some day to dry just to depreciate Her Majesty's jewels and gifts. Had King Solomon been the janitor, with all his treasures piled up in the basement, Jim would have pulled out his watch every time he passed, just to see him pluck at his beard from envy.

So now Della's beautiful hair fell about her, rippling and shining like a cascade of brown waters. She did it up again nervously and quickly. Once she faltered for a minute while a tear splashed on the worn red carpet.

On went her old brown jacket; on went her old brown hat. With a whirl of skirts and with the brilliant sparkle still in her eyes, she fluttered out the door and down the stairs to the street.

Where she stopped the sign read: "Mme. Sofronie. Hair Goods of All Kinds." One flight up Della ran, and collected herself, panting. Madame, large, too white, chilly, hardly looked the "Sofronie."

"Will you buy my hair?" asked Della.

"I buy hair," said Madame. "Take yer hat off and let's have a sight at the looks of it."

Down rippled the brown cascade.

"Twenty dollars," said Madame, lifting the mass with a practised hand.

"Give it to me quick," said Della.

Oh, and the next two hours tripped on rosy wings. Forget the hashed metaphor. She was ransacking the stores for Jim's present.

She found it at last. It surely had been made for Jim and no one else. There was no other like it in any of the stores, and she had turned all of them inside out. It was a platinum watch-chain, simple and chaste in design, properly proclaiming its value by substance alone and not by meretricious ornamentation — as all good things should do. It was even worthy of The Watch. As soon as she saw it she knew that it must be Jim's. It was like him. Quietness and value — the description applied to both. Twenty-one dollars they took from her for it, and she hurried home with the eighty-seven cents. With that chain on his watch Jim might be properly anxious about the time in any company. Grand as the watch was, he sometimes looked at it on the sly on account of the shabby old leather strap that he used in place of a proper gold chain.

When Della reached home her intoxication gave way a little to prudence and reason. She got out her curling-irons and lighted the gas and went to work repairing the ravages made by generosity added to love. Which is always a tremendous task, dear friends – a mammoth task.

Within forty minutes her head was covered with tiny close-lying curls that made her look wonderfully like a truant schoolboy. She looked at her reflection in the mirror long, carefully, and critically.

"If Jim doesn't kill me," she said to herself, "before he takes a second look at me, he'll say I look like a Coney Island chorus girl. But what could I do – oh! what could I do with a dollar and eighty-seven cents?"

At seven o'clock the coffee was made and the frying-pan was on the back of the stove, hot and ready to cook the chops.

Jim was never late. Della doubled the watch chain in her hand and sat on the corner of the table near the door that he always entered. Then she heard his step on the stair away down on the first flight, and she turned white for just a moment. She had a habit of saying little silent prayers about the simplest everyday things, and now she whispered: "Please, God, make him think I am still pretty."

The door opened and Jim stepped in and closed it. He looked thin and very serious. Poor fellow, he was only twenty-two – and had to be burdened with a family! He needed a new overcoat and he was without gloves.

Jim stepped inside the door, as immovable as a setter at the scent of quail. His eyes were fixed upon Della, and there was an expression in them that she could not read, and it terrified her. It was not anger, nor surprise, nor disapproval, nor horror, nor any of the sentiments that she had been prepared for. He simply stared at her fixedly with that peculiar expression on his face.

Della wriggled off the table and went for him.

"Jim, darling," she cried, "don't look at me that way. I had my hair cut off and sold it because I couldn't have lived through Christmas without giving you a present. It'll grow out again – you won't mind, will you? I just had to do it. My hair grows awfully fast. Say 'Merry Christmas!' Jim, and let's be happy. You don't know what a nice – what a beautiful, nice gift I've got for you."

"You've cut off your hair?" asked Jim, laboriously, as if he had not arrived at that patent fact yet even after the hardest mental labour.

"Cut it off and sold it," said Della. "Don't you like me just as well, anyhow? I'm me without my hair, ain't I?"

Jim looked about the room curiously.

"You say your hair is gone?" he said, with an air almost of idiocy.

"You needn't look for it," said Della. "It's sold, I tell you – sold and gone, too. It's Christmas Eve, boy. Be good to me, for it went for you. Maybe the hairs of my head were numbered," she went on with a sudden serious sweetness, "but nobody could ever count my love for you. Shall I put the chops on, Jim?"

Out of his trance Jim seemed to quickly wake. He enfolded his Della. For ten seconds let us regard with discreet scrutiny some inconsequential object in the other direction. Eight dollars a week or a million a year – what is the difference? A mathematician or a wit would give you the wrong answer. The Magi brought valuable gifts, but that was not among them. This dark assertion will be illuminated later on.

Jim drew a package from his overcoat pocket and threw it upon the table.

"Don't make any mistake, Dell," he said, "about me. I don't think there's anything in the way of a haircut or a shave or a shampoo that could make me like my girl any less. But if you'll unwrap that package you may see why you had me going awhile at first."

White fingers and nimble tore at the string and paper. And then an ecstatic scream of joy; and then, alas! a quick feminine change to hysterical tears and wails, necessitating the immediate employment of all the comforting powers of the lord of the flat.

The Gift of the Magi

For there lay The Combs – the set of combs that Della had worshipped for long in a Broadway window. Beautiful combs, pure tortoise shell, with jewelled rims – just the shade to wear in the beautiful vanished hair. They were expensive combs, she knew, and her heart had simply craved and yearned over them without the least hope of possession. And now they were hers, but the tresses that should have adorned the coveted adornments were gone.

But she hugged them to her bosom, and at length she was able to look up with dim eyes and a smile and say: "My hair grows so fast, Jim!"

And then Della leaped up like a little singed cat and cried, "Oh, oh!"

Jim had not yet seen his beautiful present. She held it out to him eagerly upon her open palm. The dull precious metal seemed to flash with a reflection of her ardent spirit.

"Isn't it a dandy, Jim? I hunted all over town to find it. You'll have to look at the time a hundred times a day now. Give me your watch. I want to see how it looks on it."

Instead of obeying, Jim tumbled down on the couch and put his hands under the back of his head and smiled.

"Dell," said he, "let's put our Christmas presents away and keep 'em awhile. They're too nice to use just at present. I sold the watch to get the money to buy your combs. And now suppose you put the chops on."

The Magi, as you know, were wise men – wonderfully wise men – who brought gifts to the Babe in the manger. They invented the art of giving Christmas presents. Being wise, their gifts were no doubt wise ones, possibly bearing the privilege of exchange in case of duplication. And here I have lamely related to you the uneventful chronicle of two foolish children in a flat who most unwisely sacrificed for each other the greatest treasures of their house. But in a last word to the wise of these days let it be said that of all who give gifts these two were the wisest. Of all who give and receive gifts, such as they are the wisest. Everywhere they are the wisest. They are the Magi.

THE CHRISTMAS CUCKOO

Frances Browne

Once upon a time there stood in the midst of a bleak moor, in the north country, a certain village. All its inhabitants were poor, for their fields were barren and they had little trade; but the poorest of them all were two brothers called Scrub and Spare, who followed the cobbler's craft and had but one stall between them. It was a hut built of clay and wattles. The door was low and always open by day, for there was no window. The roof did not entirely keep out the rain and the only thing comfortable about it was a wide hearth, for which the brothers could never find wood enough to make a sufficient fire. There they worked in most brotherly friendship, though with little encouragement.

The people of that village were not extravagant in shoes, and better cobblers than Scrub and Spare might be found. Spiteful people said there were no shoes so bad that they would not be worse for their mending. Nevertheless Scrub and Spare managed to live, between their own trade, a small barley-field and a cottage garden, till one unlucky day when a new cobbler arrived in the village. He had lived in the capital city of the kingdom, and by his own account cobbled for the queen and the princesses. His awls were sharp, his lasts were new; he set up his stall in a neat cottage with two windows. The villagers soon found out that one patch of his would wear two of the brothers'. In short, all the mending left Scrub and

Spare and went to the new cobbler. The season had been wet and cold, their barley did not ripen well and the cabbages never half closed in the garden. So the brothers were poor that winter, and when Christmas came they had nothing to feast on but a barley loaf, a piece of rusty bacon and some small beer of their own brewing. Worse than that, the snow was very deep and they could get no firewood. Their hut stood at the end of the village and beyond it spread the bleak moor, now all white and silent; but that moor had once been a forest and great roots of old trees were still to be found in it, loosened from the soil and laid bare by the winds and rains — one of these, a rough, gnarled log, lay hard by their door, the half of it above the snow, and Spare said to his brother:

"Shall we sit here cold on Christmas while the great root lies yonder? Let us chop it up for firewood; the work will make us warm."

"No," said Scrub; "it's not right to chop wood on Christmas; besides, that root is too hard to be broken with any hatchet."

"Hard or not, we must have a fire," replied Spare. "Come, brother, help me in with it. Poor as we are, there is nobody in the village will have such a yule log as ours."

Scrub liked a little grandeur, and in hopes of having a fine yule log both brothers strained and strove with all their might till, between pulling and pushing, the great old root was safe on the hearth and beginning to crackle and blaze with the red embers. In high glee the cobblers sat down to their beer and bacon. The door was shut, for there was nothing but cold moonlight and snow outside; but the hut, strewn with fir boughs, and ornamented with holly, looked cheerful as the ruddy blaze flared up and rejoiced their hearts.

"Long life and good fortune to ourselves, brother!" said Spare. "I hope you will drink that toast, and may we never have a worse fire on Christmas — but what is that?"

Spare set down the drinking-horn, and the brothers listened astonished, for out of the blazing root they heard, "Cuckoo! cuckoo!" as plain as ever the spring-bird's voice came over the moor on a May morning.

"It is something bad," said Scrub, terribly frightened.

"Maybe not," said Spare; and out of the deep hole at the side which the fire had not reached flew a large grey cuckoo, and lit on the table before them. Much as the cobblers had been surprised, they were still more so when it said:

"Good gentlemen, what season is this?"

"It's Christmas," said Spare.

"Then a merry Christmas to you!" said the cuckoo. "I went to sleep in the hollow of that old root one evening last summer and never woke till the heat of your fire made me think it was summer again; but now, since you have burned my lodging, let me stay in your hut till the spring comes round – I only want a hole to sleep in, and when I go on my travels next summer be assured I will bring you some present for your trouble."

"Stay, and welcome," said Spare, while Scrub sat wondering if it were something bad or not; "I'll make you a good warm hole in the thatch. But you must be hungry after that long sleep. Here is a slice of barley bread. Come, help us to keep Christmas!"

The cuckoo ate up the slice, drank water from the brown jug, for he would take no beer, and flew into a snug hole which Spare scooped for him in the thatch of the hut.

Scrub said he was afraid it wouldn't be lucky; but as it slept on and the days passed he forgot his fears. So the snow melted, the heavy rains came, the cold grew less, the days lengthened, and one sunny morning the brothers were awakened by the cuckoo shouting its own cry to let them know the spring had come.

"Now I'm going on my travels," said the bird, "over the world to tell men of the spring. There is no country where trees bud or flowers bloom that I will not cry in before the year goes round. Give me another slice of barley bread to keep me on my journey and tell me what present I shall bring you at the twelvemonth's end."

Scrub would have been angry with his brother for cutting so large a slice, their store of barley-meal being low; but his mind was occupied with what present would be most prudent to ask: at length a lucky thought struck him.

"Good master cuckoo," said he, "if a great traveller who sees all the world like you, could know of any place where diamonds or pearls were to be found, one of a tolerable size brought in your beak would help such poor men as my brother and I to provide something better than barley bread for your next entertainment."

"I know nothing of diamonds or pearls," said the cuckoo; "they are in the hearts of rocks and the sands of rivers. My knowledge is only of that which grows on the earth. But there are two trees hard by the well that lies at the world's end: one of them is called the golden tree, for its leaves are all of beaten gold; every winter they fall into the well with a sound like scattered coin, and I know not what becomes of them. As for the other, it is always green like a laurel. Some call it the wise, and some the merry tree. Its leaves never fall, but they that get one of them keep a blithe heart in spite of all misfortunes and can make themselves as merry in a hut as in a palace."

"Good master cuckoo, bring me a leaf off that tree!" cried Spare.

"Now, brother, don't be a fool!" said Scrub. "Think of the leaves of beaten gold! Dear master cuckoo, bring me one of them!"

Before another word could be spoken, the cuckoo had flown out of the open door, and was shouting its spring cry over moor and meadow. The brothers were poorer than ever that year; nobody would send them a single shoe to mend. The new cobbler said in scorn they should come to be his apprentices; and Scrub and Spare would have left the village but for their barley-field, their cabbage garden and a certain maid called Fairfeather, whom both the cobblers had courted for seven years without even knowing which she meant to favour.

Sometimes Fairfeather seemed inclined to Scrub, sometimes she smiled on Spare; but the brothers never disputed for that. They sowed their barley, planted their cabbage and, now that their trade was gone, worked in the rich villagers' fields to make out a scanty living. So the seasons came and passed: spring, summer, harvest and winter followed each other as they have done from the beginning. At the end of the last, Scrub and Spare had grown so poor and ragged that Fairfeather thought them beneath her notice. Old neighbours forgot to invite them to wedding feasts or merrymaking; and they thought the cuckoo had forgotten them too, when at daybreak, on the first of April, they heard a hard beak knocking at their door and a voice crying:

"Cuckoo! cuckoo! Let me in with my presents."

Spare ran to open the door, and in came the cuckoo, carrying on one side of his bill a golden leaf larger than that of any tree in the north country; and in the other, one like that of the common laurel, only it had a fresher green.

"Here," it said, giving the gold to Scrub and the green to Spare, "it is a long carriage from the world's end. Give me a slice of barley bread, for I must tell the north country that the spring has come."

Scrub did not grudge the thickness of that slice, though it was cut from their last loaf. So much gold had never been in the cobbler's hands before and he could not help exulting over his brother.

"See the wisdom of my choice!" he said, holding up the large leaf of gold. "As for yours, as good might be plucked from any hedge. I wonder a sensible bird would carry the like so far."

"Good master cobbler," cried the cuckoo, finishing the slice, "your conclusions are more hasty than courteous. If your brother be disappointed this time, I go on the same journey every year, and for your hospitable entertainment will think it no trouble to bring each of you whichever leaf you desire."

"Darling cuckoo," cried Scrub, "bring me a golden one"; and Spare, looking up from the green leaf on which he gazed as though it were a crown jewel, said:

"Be sure to bring me one from the merry tree," and away flew the cuckoo.

"This is the Feast of All Fools, and it ought to be your birthday," said Scrub. "Did ever man fling away such an opportunity of getting rich! Much good your merry leaves will do in the midst of rags and poverty!" So he went on, but Spare laughed at him and answered with quaint old proverbs concerning the cares that come with gold, till Scrub, at length getting angry, vowed his brother was not fit to live with a respectable man; and taking his lasts, his awls and his golden leaf, he left the wattle hut and went to tell the villagers.

They were astonished at the folly of Spare and charmed with Scrub's good sense, particularly when he showed them the golden leaf, and told that the cuckoo would bring him one every spring. The new cobbler immediately took him into partnership, the greatest people sent him their shoes to mend. Fairfeather smiled graciously upon him and in the course of that summer they were married, with a grand wedding feast, at which the whole village danced, except Spare, who was not invited, because the bride could not bear his low-mindedness, and his brother thought him a disgrace to the family.

Indeed all who heard the story concluded that Spare must be mad, and nobody would associate with him but a lame tinker, a beggar-boy and a poor woman reputed to be a witch because she was old and ugly. As for Scrub, he established himself with Fairfeather in a cottage close by that of the new cobbler, and quite as fine. There he mended shoes to everybody's satisfaction, had a scarlet coat for holidays and a fat goose for dinner every wedding-day. Fairfeather too had a crimson gown and fine blue ribands; but neither she nor Scrub were content, for to buy this grandeur the golden leaf had to be broken and parted with piece by piece, so the last morsel was gone before the cuckoo came with another.

Spare lived on in the old hut, and worked in the cabbage garden. (Scrub had got the barley-field because he was the elder.) Every day his coat grew more ragged, and the hut more weatherbeaten; but people remarked that he never looked sad nor sour; and the wonder was that, from the time they began to keep his company, the tinker grew kinder to the

179

poor ass with which he travelled the country, the beggar-boy kept out of mischief and the old woman was never cross to her cat or angry with the children.

Every first of April the cuckoo came tapping at their doors with the golden leaf to Scrub and the green to Spare. Fairfeather would have entertained him nobly with wheaten bread and honey, for she had some notion of persuading him to bring two gold leaves instead of one; but the cuckoo flew away to eat barley bread with Spare, saying he was not fit company for fine people, and liked the old hut where he slept so snugly from Christmas till spring.

Scrub spent the golden leaves, and Spare kept the merry ones; and I know not how many years passed in this manner, when a certain great lord who owned that village came to the neighbourhood. His castle stood on the moor. It was ancient and strong, with high towers and a deep moat. All the country, as far as one could see from the highest turret, belonged to its lord; but he had not been there for twenty years, and would not have come then, only he was melancholy. The cause of his grief was that he had been prime minister at court and in high favour, till somebody told the crown prince that he had spoken disrespectfully concerning the turning out of his royal highness's toes, and of the king that he did not lay on taxes enough, whereon the north country lord was turned out of office and banished to his own estate. There he lived for some weeks in very bad temper. The servants said nothing would please him, and the villagers put on their worst clothes lest he should raise their rents; but one day in the harvest time his lordship chanced to meet Spare gathering watercresses at a meadow stream, and fell into talk with the cobbler.

How it was nobody could tell, but from the hour of that discourse the great lord cast away his melancholy: he forgot his lost office and his court enemies, the king's taxes and the crown prince's toes, and went about with a noble train, hunting, fishing and making merry in his hall, where all travellers were entertained and all the poor were welcome.

This strange story spread through the north country, and great company came to the cobbler's hut – rich men who had lost their money, poor men who had lost their friends, beauties who had grown old, wits who had gone out of fashion – all came to talk with Spare, and whatever their troubles had been, all went home merry. The rich gave him presents, the poor gave him thanks. Spare's coat ceased to be ragged, he had bacon with his cabbage and the villagers began to think there was some sense in him.

By this time his fame had reached the capital city, and even the court. There were a great many discontented people there besides the king, who had lately fallen into ill humour because a neighbouring princess, with seven islands for her dowry, would not marry his eldest son. So a royal messenger was sent to Spare, with a velvet mantle, a diamond ring and a command that he should repair to court immediately.

"Tomorrow is the first of April," said Spare, "and I will go with you two hours after sunrise."

The messenger lodged all night at the castle, and the cuckoo came at sunrise with the merry leaf.

"Court is a fine place," he said when the cobbler told him he was going, "but I cannot come there, they would lay snares and catch me; so be careful of the leaves I have brought you, and give me a farewell slice of barley bread."

Spare was sorry to part with the cuckoo, little as he had of his company; but he gave him a slice which would have broken Scrub's heart in former times, it was so thick and large; and having sewed up the leaves in the lining of his leather doublet, he set out with the messenger on his way to court.

His coming caused great surprise there. Everybody wondered what the king could see in such a common-looking man; but scarce had his majesty conversed with him half an hour, when the princess and her seven islands were forgotten, and orders given that a feast for all comers should be spread in the banquet hall. The princes of the blood, the great lords and ladies, ministers of state and judges of the land, after that, discoursed with Spare, and the more they talked the lighter grew their hearts, so that such changes had never been seen at court. The lords forgot their spites and the ladies their envies, the princes and ministers made friends among themselves, and the judges showed no favour.

As for Spare, he had a chamber assigned him in the palace and a seat at the king's table; one sent him rich robes and another costly jewels; but in the midst of all his grandeur he still wore the leathern doublet, which the palace servants thought remarkably mean. One day the king's attention being drawn to it by the chief page, his majesty inquired why Spare didn't give it to a beggar? But the cobbler answered:

"High and mighty monarch, this doublet was with me before silk and velvet came – I find it easier to wear than the court cut; moreover it serves to keep me humble, by recalling the days when it was my holiday garment."

The king thought this a wise speech, and commanded that no one should find fault with the leathern doublet. So things went, till tidings of his brother's good fortune reached Scrub in the moorland cottage on another first of April, when the cuckoo came with two golden leaves, because he had none to carry for Spare.

"Think of that!" said Fairfeather. "Here we are spending our lives in this humdrum place, and Spare making his fortune at court with two or three paltry green leaves! What would they say to our golden ones? Let us pack up and make our way to the king's palace; I'm sure he will make you a lord and me a lady of honour, not to speak of all the fine clothes and presents we shall have.'

Scrub thought this excellent reasoning, and their packing up began; but it was soon found that the cottage contained few things fit for carrying to court. Fairfeather could not think of her wooden bowls, spoons and trenchers being seen there. Scrub considered his lasts and awls better left behind, as without them, he concluded, no one would suspect him of being a cobbler. So putting on their holiday clothes, Fairfeather took her looking-glass and Scrub his drinking-horn, which happened to have a very thin rim of silver, and each carrying a golden leaf carefully wrapped up that none might see it till they reached the palace, the pair set out in great expectation.

How far Scrub and Fairfeather journeyed I cannot say, but when the sun was high and warm at noon, they came into a wood both tired and hungry.

"If I had known it was so far to court," said Scrub, "I would have brought the end of that barley loaf which we left in the cupboard."

"Husband," said Fairfeather, "you shouldn't have such mean thoughts: how could one eat barley bread on the way to a palace? Let us rest ourselves under this tree, and look at our golden leaves to see if they are safe." In looking at the leaves, and talking of their fine prospects, Scrub and Fairfeather did not perceive that a very thin old woman had slipped from behind the tree, with a long staff in her hand and a great wallet by her side.

"Noble lord and lady," she said, "for I know you are such by your voices, though my eyes are dim and my hearing none of the sharpest, will you condescend to tell me where I may find some water to mix a bottle of mead which I carry in my wallet, because it is too strong for me?"

As the old woman spoke, she pulled out a large wooden bottle such as shepherds used in the ancient times, corked with leaves rolled together and having a small wooden cup hanging from its handle.

"Perhaps you will do me the favour to taste," she said. "It is only made of the best honey. I have also cream cheese and a wheaten loaf here, if such honourable persons as you would eat the like."

Scrub and Fairfeather became very condescending after this speech. They were now sure that there must be some appearance of nobility about them; besides, they were very hungry, and having hastily wrapped up the golden leaves, they assured the old woman they were not at all proud, notwithstanding the lands and castles they had left behind them in the north country, and would willingly help to lighten the wallet. The old woman could scarcely be persuaded to sit down for pure humility, but at length she did, and before the wallet was half empty Scrub and Fairfeather firmly believed that there must be something remarkably noble-looking about them. This was not entirely owing to her ingenious discourse. The old woman was a wood-witch; her name was Buttertongue; and all her time was spent in making mead, which being boiled with curious herbs and spells, had the power of making all who drank it fall asleep and dream with their eyes open. She had two dwarfs of sons; one was named Spy and the other Pounce. Wherever their mother went they were not far behind; and whoever tasted her mead was sure to be robbed by the dwarfs.

Scrub and Fairfeather sat leaning against the old tree. The cobbler had a lump of cheese in his hand; his wife held fast a hunch of bread. Their eyes and mouths were both open, but they were dreaming of great grandeur at court, when the old woman raised her shrill voice:

"What ho, my sons, come here and carry home the harvest!"

No sooner had she spoken than the two little dwarfs darted out of the neighbouring thicket.

"Idle boys!" cried the mother. "What have you done today to help our living?"

"I have been to the city," said Spy, "and could see nothing. These are hard times for us – everybody minds his business so contentedly since that cobbler came; but here is a leathern doublet which his page threw out of the window; it's of no use, but I brought it to let you see I was not idle." And he tossed down Spare's doublet, with the merry leaves in it, which he had carried like a bundle on his little back.

To explain how Spy came by it, I must tell you that the forest was not far from the great city where Spare lived in such high esteem. All things had gone well with the cobbler till the king thought it was quite unbecoming to see such a worthy man without a servant. His majesty, therefore, to let all men understand his royal favour towards Spare, appointed

one of his own pages to wait upon him. The name of this youth was Tinseltoes, and though he was the seventh of the king's pages nobody in all the court had grander notions. Nothing could please him that had not gold or silver about it, and his grandmother feared he would hang himself for being appointed page to a cobbler. As for Spare, if anything could have troubled him, this token of his majesty's kindness would have done it.

The honest man had been so used to serve himself that the page was always in the way, but his merry leaves came to his assistance; and, to the great surprise of his grandmother, Tinseltoes took wonderfully to the new service. Some said it was because Spare gave him nothing to do but play at bowls all day on the palace green. Yet one thing grieved the heart of Tinseltoes, and that was his master's leathern doublet; but for it, he was persuaded, people would never remember that Spare had been a cobbler, and the page took a deal of pains to let him see how unfashionable it was at court; but Spare answered Tinseltoes as he had done the king, and at last, finding nothing better would do, the page got up one fine morning earlier than his master, and tossed the leathern doublet out of the back window into a certain lane where Spy found it, and brought it to his mother.

"That nasty thing!" said the old woman. "Where is the good in it?"

By this time Pounce had taken everything of value from Scrub and Fairfeather – the looking glass, the silver-rimmed horn, the husband's scarlet coat, the wife's gay mantle, and above all the golden leaves, which so rejoiced old Butter-tongue and her sons that they threw the leathern doublet over the sleeping cobbler for a jest, and went off to their hut in the heart of the forest.

The sun was going down when Scrub and Fairfeather awoke from dreaming that they had been made a lord and a lady and sat clothed in silk and velvet, feasting with the king in his palace hall. It was a great disappointment to find their golden leaves and all their best things gone. Scrub tore his hair and vowed to take the old woman's life, while Fair-feather lamented sore; but Scrub, feeling cold for want of his coat, put on the leathern doublet without asking or caring whence it came.

Scarcely was it buttoned on when a change came over him; he addressed such merry discourse to Fairfeather, that, instead of lamentations, she made the wood ring with laughter. Both busied themselves in getting up a hut of boughs, in which Scrub kindled a fire with a flint and steel, which, together with his pipe, he had brought unknown to Fairfeather, who had told him the like was never heard of at court. Then they found a pheasant's nest at the root of an old oak, made a meal of roasted eggs, and went to sleep on a heap of long green grass which they had gathered, with nightingales singing all night long in the old trees about them. So it happened that Scrub and Fairfeather stayed day after day in the forest, making their hut larger and more comfortable against the winter, living on wild birds' eggs and berries and never thinking of their lost golden leaves, or their journey to court.

In the meantime Spare had got up and missed his doublet. Tinseltoes, of course, said he knew nothing about it. The whole palace was searched, and every servant questioned, till all the court wondered why such a fuss was made about an old leathern doublet. That very day things came back to their old fashion. Quarrels began among the lords and jealousies among the ladies. The king said his subjects did not pay him half enough taxes, the queen wanted more jewels, the servants took to their old bickerings and got up some new ones. Spare found himself getting wonderfully dull, and very much out of place: nobles began to ask what business a cobbler had at the king's table, and his majesty ordered the palace chronicles to be searched for a precedent. The cobbler was too wise to tell all he had lost with that doublet, but being by this time somewhat familiar with court customs, he proclaimed a reward of fifty gold pieces to any who would bring him news concerning it.

Scarcely was this made known in the city when the gates and outer courts of the palace were filled with men, women and children, some bringing leathern doublets of every cut and colour – some with tales of what they had heard and seen in their walks about the neighbourhood. And so much news concerning all sorts of great people came out of these stories that lords and ladies ran to the king with complaints of Spare as a speaker of slander; and his majesty, being now satisfied that there was no example in all the palace records of such a retainer, issued a decree banishing the cobbler for ever from court and confiscating all his goods in favour of Tinseltoes.

That royal edict was scarcely published before the page was in full possession of his rich chamber, his costly garments and all the presents the courtiers had given him; while Spare, having no longer the fifty pieces of gold to give, was glad to make his escape out of the back window, for fear of the nobles, who vowed to be revenged on him, and the crowd, who were prepared to stone him for cheating them about his doublet.

The window from which Spare let himself down with a strong rope was that from which Tinseltoes had tossed the doublet, and as the cobbler came down late in the twilight, a poor woodman with a heavy load of faggots stopped and stared at him in great astonishment.

"What's the matter, friend?" said Spare. "Did you never see a man coming down from a back window before?"

"Why," said the woodman, "the last morning I passed here a leathern doublet came out of that very window, and I'll be bound you are the owner of it."

"That I am, friend," said the cobbler. "Can you tell me which way that doublet went?"

"As I walked on," said the woodman, "a dwarf, called Spy, bundled it up and ran off to his mother in the forest."

"Honest friend," said Spare, taking off the last of his fine clothes (a grass-green mantle edged with gold), "I'll give you this if you will follow the dwarf and bring me back my doublet."

"It would not be good to carry faggots in," said the

woodman. "But if you want back your doublet, the road to the forest lies at the end of this lane," and he trudged away.

Determined to find his doublet, and sure that neither crowd nor courtiers could catch him in the forest, Spare went on his way, and was soon among the tall trees; but neither hut nor dwarf could he see. Moreover the night came on; the wood was dark and tangled, but here and there the moon shone through its alleys, the great owls flitted about, and the nightingales sang. So he went on, hoping to find some place of shelter. At last the red light of a fire, gleaming through a thicket, led him to the door of a low hut. It stood half open, as if there was nothing to fear, and within he saw his brother Scrub snoring loudly on a bed of grass, at the foot of which lay his own leathern doublet; while Fairfeather, in a kirtle made of plaited rushes, sat roasting pheasant's eggs by the fire.

"Good evening, mistress," said Spare, stepping in.

The blaze shone on him, but so changed was her brother-in-law with his court life, that Fairfeather did not know him, and she answered far more courteously than was her wont.

"Good evening, master. Whence come ye so late? But speak low, for my good man has sorely tired himself cleaving wood, and is taking a sleep, as you see, before supper."

"A good rest to him," said Spare, perceiving he was not known. "I come from the court for a day's hunting, and have lost my way in the forest."

"Sit down and have a share of our supper," said Fair-feather. "I will put some more eggs in the ashes; and tell me the news of court — I used to think of it long ago when I was young and foolish."

"Did you never go there?" said the cobbler. "So fair a dame as you would make the ladies marvel."

"You are pleased to flatter," said Fairfeather; "but my husband has a brother there, and we left our moorland village to try our fortune also. An old woman enticed us with fair words and strong drink at the entrance of this forest, where we fell asleep and dreamt of great things; but when we woke, everything had been robbed from us — my looking-glass, my scarlet cloak, my husband's Sunday coat; and, in place of all, the robbers left him that old leathern doublet, which he has worn ever since, and never was so merry in all his life, though we live in this poor hut."

"It is a shabby doublet, that," said Spare, taking up the garment, and seeing that it was his own, for the merry leaves were still sewed in its lining. "It would be good for hunting in, however – your husband would be glad to part with it, I dare say, in exchange for this handsome cloak"; and he pulled off the green mantle and buttoned on the doublet, much to Fairfeather's delight, who ran and shook Scrub, crying:

"Husband! husband! rise and see what a good bargain I have made!"

Scrub gave one closing snore, and muttered something about the root being hard; but he rubbed his eyes, gazed up at his brother, and said:

"Spare, is that really you? How did you like the court, and have you made your fortune?"

"That I have, brother," said Spare, "in getting back my own good leathern doublet. Come, let us eat eggs and rest ourselves here this night. In the morning we will return to our own old hut, at the end of the moorland village where the Christmas Cuckoo will come and bring us leaves."

Scrub and Fairfeather agreed. So in the morning they all returned, and found the old hut none the worse for wear and weather. The neighbours came about them to ask the news of court, and see if they had made their fortune. Everybody was astonished to find the three poorer than ever, but somehow they liked to go back to the hut. Spare brought out the lasts and awls he had hidden in a corner; Scrub and he began their old trade, and the whole north country found out that there never were such cobblers.

They mended the shoes of lords and ladies as well as the common people; everybody was satisfied. Their custom increased from day to day, and all that were disappointed, discontented or unlucky came to the hut as in old times before Spare went to court.

The rich brought them presents, the poor did them service. The hut itself changed, no one knew how. Flowering honeysuckle grew over its roof; red and white roses grew thick about its door. Moreover the Christmas Cuckoo always came on the first of April, bringing three leaves of the merry tree – for Scrub and Fairfeather would have no more golden ones. So it was with them when I last heard the news of the north country.

ACKNOWLEDGEMENTS

Our thanks are due to the undermentioned publishers, agents and authors for permission to include the following material:

A. M. Heath and Company Ltd for *Christmas with the Chrystals* by Noel Streatfeild.
Hodder & Stoughton Education for *The Story of Brother Johannick and his Silver Bell* (from *Tales for Jack and Jane*) by Elizabeth Clark.
Roy Fuller for *The Real True Father Christmas*.
The author and Juvenilia Literary Agency for *The Ghost of Christmas Present* by Wendy Eyton, originally published by Frederick Warne (Publishers).
Leon Garfield for *The Forbidden Child*.
J. M. Dent & Sons Ltd for *The Chistmas Cherries* by Chrétien de Troyes, translated by John Hampden (from *Sir William and the Wolf and Other Stories* Children's Illustrated Classics Series).
Brian Alderson for *The Day We Threw the Switch on Georgie Tozer*.
Mary Small for *Christmas and Peter Moss*.
Diana Ross for *The Weathercock's Carol*.
We are grateful to the Children's Librarians of the London Borough of Barnet; Mary Junor, Schools' Librarian, Barnet; and the Librarians of Hendon, Golders Green and Child's Hill for their ever-ready help.
To Phyllis Hunt, Editor of Children's Books at Faber and Faber, it is difficult to express adequately our gratitude for her tireless attention to detail at all points and our appreciation of her scholarly help, and we should also like to thank her colleagues for their invaluable assistance over every aspect of our books.